PENGUIN BOOKS

DEAD COLLECTIONS

Sarah Jung

Isaac Fellman is the author of *The Breath of the Sun* (published under his pre-transition first name), which won the 2019 Lambda Literary Award for LGBT Science Fiction, Fantasy, and Horror. He is an archivist at a queer historical society in San Francisco.

DEAD COLLECTIONS

Isaac Fellman

PENGUIN BOOKS

PENGUIN BOOKS
An imprint of Penguin Random House LLC
penguinrandomhouse.com

LIBRARY OF CONGRESS CATALOGING-IN-PUBLICATION DATA
Names: Fellman, Isaac R., author.
Title: Dead collections / Isaac Fellman.
Description: [New York] : Penguin Books, [2022]
Identifiers: LCCN 2021011936 (print) | LCCN 2021011937 (ebook) |
ISBN 9780143136910 (paperback) | ISBN 9780525508403 (ebook)
Classification: LCC PS3606.E38848 D43 2022 (print) |
LCC PS3606.E38848 (ebook) | DDC 813/.6—dc23
LC record available at https://lccn.loc.gov/2021011936
LC ebook record available at https://lccn.loc.gov/2021011937

Printed in the United States of America
1st Printing

Set in ITC Founders Caslon Twelve
Designed by Sabrina Bowers

The collector is an honest lone vampire; the archivist is a licensed vampire.

—ANDREI CODRESCU, *Bibliodeath*

DEAD COLLECTIONS

CHAPTER 1

A Slow Event

When I was training to become an archivist, my mentor told me, "A thing is just a slow event." The line wasn't hers, but it struck me with the needle-prick of originality. A slow event. A person is that too, an event seventy or eighty years long, very complex, hundreds of systems, iron and nitrogen and oxygen, blood flowing into blood.

This story is a mystery of sorts, although most mysteries begin with a dead body. That's a thing whose event is nearly done, with its last climaxes soon to come. The dead body is always pretty rude. It comes into your life and reminds you of the joke at the end; it ruins your appetite, it ruins your day. There are no dead bodies in archives—except maybe for mine. Oh, sometimes there are ashes, and a few times bones, and there's often quite a lot of hair, but in general what you find in archives is the *absence* of a body, the chalk outline of a life, crowded all around with papers and artifacts and ephemera, but with a terribly small hollowness within. You can almost taste the closeness of the body sometimes, almost feel the glossy heat of it, but never quite. It's cold in the archives, and there's nobody there. I belong in the archives. I am cold too.

As that day began, I was soaking my hands in hot water until they got warm enough for me to shake someone else's. I jammed one and then the other into my Styrofoam cup, and with the hand that wasn't soaking, I kept trying and failing to get my phone to acknowledge my fingerprint. When it's warm enough for the button to work, that's how I know it's warm enough for a handshake, plus I wanted to read my phone.

I didn't see myself as being in the closet about my illness, my vampirism, but I'd only ever told my boss and HR. As for telling visitors, it felt too private to explain, especially early in the morning, in a room where the guests aren't even allowed coffee. So I'd give them a mock-up of life, immersing my hands in the water until they took on its warmth like rubber does, and putting on gloves when I handled photographs in front of visitors, although my fingers make no prints.

My coworkers also didn't know that I lived down here, and for that matter, neither did HR. There was a couch in my office where I would sometimes lie down for what passes for my sleep; there was a vivid network of bars, all-night coffee shops, and wet sugary streets in which I could take my greedy sips of fresh air at night. I do drink, you see, and I do breathe. And I can eat if I want, but only the strongest foods make any impression on my burned-out taste buds, and of course none of them nourish me. They tend to be the preserved foods—strong kimchi, pungent cheese, ultra-sweet jams and jellies. I'm all about preservation. I never meant to become such a walking stereotype, but I love my work.

Someday, I will write all this down. For now, I prefer it in my head, where it's mutable and fresh as clay. I prefer to remember this story between one bright moment and the next of an increasingly crowded life. It's not an old story yet, and I am still figuring out what it means.

I used to be an archivist at the Historical Society of Northern California. The society is in the basement of a building on Market Street, a basement whose generous toilet was always on the edge of overflowing, and which had mice but not rats. The rooms were really designed to be storerooms. I had an office, by virtue of my seniority, which was just off the main workroom and fifty feet from the vault; the director's office was next door. She was off on maternity leave, so I was in charge. The carpet was thinly striped in maroon and beige, clotted with dust and crud and rusty staples. The walls between the offices and the vault didn't have any tops to them. You could bung a penny or a plasticlip right over them, and I have, late at night after everyone's gone home.

Every day I felt the city's palpable weight. There was a ten-story building above us, sealing the daylight out like a stamp, but it felt sometimes like fifty stories, a hundred stories. I would come out at night almost dazed that the city was so small. In my mind, it all grew to monstrous height above me, rootless and dazzling.

The elevator dinged outside the archives' door. Normally at that point you heard an anxious *hup*, the sound of someone turning our gritty steel doorknob, unsure whether the archives can even be in here—in this vinegar-smelling hallway like a conduit for acid, like a long-abandoned part of the body. Elsie turned it with confidence, like staff. But when she was inside, her hands were hesitant, and she looked around the same way most people do at first: slow and wondering, with more *up* in the look than usual. Our ceiling's low, but people always do look up, as if they're worried about the weight of the city too.

It's hard to remember my first impressions of Elsie, who has become so familiar to me that those memories are all worn away like stones in a watery cave. First impressions are strange things. I believe in them the way I believe in fortune-telling. What, then, did she portend?

I think she was all stiffness and solidity. A tall woman, big, in a stiff green velvet dress whose skirt stood out from her hips. Some big women are loose and soft, with a creamy invitingness—I mean not of attitude or personality, but a co-incidence of how their body's built. Elsie's body was of denser stuff, and her face was matte and inexpressive, and her brown hair in a curly bob was very much "done." I read her as about my age, forty-one, though I look much younger than I am and it turned out that she looked a little older. Her fingernails were matte too, kept short but manicured in black, and when her hand met mine, it was if it had slipped beneath that painstakingly warmed skin and peeled it off. She was shaking raw muscle, and her hand was much colder than mine. Her shake was weak, her hands soft.

Where had this jolt come from, this shot to the heart? I saw my little office through her polite eyes: the jar of bitten pencils, the trash can full of water-damaged folders. On the wall was a panel from an old exhibit, *Blood: The Last Hundred Years*—a paragraph of absurdly somber text, headlined "Vampirism: 'The Thirsty Sickness.'"

I motioned her to the sofa and all at once I was aware that it was the sofa where I slept. It seemed suddenly inappropriate, even with my nubbly electric blanket folded away and sitting on my piano keyboard, the cord still protruding down and plugged into the wall. I like things tidy and efficient, although I do very little with the time I save.

"So I think I told you that I've been planning to donate my wife's things," she said, prompting me. I must really have been sitting still for the full length of that paragraph, dazed and breathing my reflexive breaths. It takes the body a long time to forget that it doesn't need to breathe anymore; I know very senior vampires who still do.

"Yes, well," I said, and I launched into an explanation that's not relevant here: our collection policy, how we decide what to accession, committees, my absent boss. Then I snapped protocol like a rubber band and added, "Of course, we'll say yes. For a collection like this, that's just a formality—the only objection I could *imagine* is that it's a bit out of scope, since Tracy lived in Los Angeles for most of her life, and she went to USC, and no doubt they'd be very interested in her papers."

"But we've been in Marin forever," she said. "And she wrote *The Black Kite* in Marin, and *The Black Kite* is how she wanted to be remembered."

"I'm sorry—*The Black Kite*?"

"Her novel," said Elsie, as if I ought to know. Then there was a faint embarrassed shifting whose source I couldn't determine. Her hands? Her breath? Something deeper in the body that showed itself only in a twitch of the skin? "She's been writing it for the past seven years. I think it was almost done, but she didn't want to show more than a few paragraphs to anyone, even me. The whole time she was dying, I expected her to show it to me, or to give me some idea of what to do with it. But she didn't."

"So typically an archivist will want you to donate the copyrights to the work, so that if we lose touch with the heirs, we can still publish parts of things, or give permission."

"Oh, that's fine. I never want to see this stuff again." She went rigid for a moment and looked down. "I'm sorry if I sound callous. It's just that I feel her presence, and it makes me so tired."

"People tell me that sometimes."

"They do? Why do you think it is?"

"Loss of context," I said. "That's what I think. When I take in a new collection, every tchotchke and every line of text feels like it's been soaked in meaning but left to dry out. So what's left is just a color, and a mark, and maybe a smell, but what the liquid was is impossible to tell. You can't know why they kept these things, and you drive yourself nuts trying to understand what was in their mind. It reminds us that we can't know our loved ones' minds."

"Oh," said Elsie, her face collapsing into a smile, "I knew her mind just fine."

"Well, I mean," I said, "I'm also an idiot."

"No, you're clearly not. But you didn't know Tracy. She had a mind that you had no choice but to live inside—not that she was a cruel person, an abusive person—but she was a very fully realized person. And it got worse when she died. Tracy *alive* was like dating a boa constrictor, or that Norse snake whose body is the world. Tracy dead is like dating nitrogen or hydrogen. She's in every particle of air. I'm sorry," she added.

She wasn't apologizing for her words, but for a rough flurry of tears that had broken through her smile, and I poked the tissues on my desk and she took three in loud, quick succession. She wasn't doing that tender little dab-crying women in makeup do. She was mopping her eyes, blowing her nose, sobbing.

I went to get her a glass of water, although there were archival papers in my office. I just couldn't bear to watch her cry without doing anything more. She took it when I nudged it into her hand; she drank it with her hand over her eyes, like an initiation. Then our eyes met, mine dry and hers wet and mascara-softened, and she said, "Thank you."

"People cry in here all the time."

"You know, in another life, maybe I would've been a librarian," she said into the cup. "Do people tell you that a lot too?"

"Yes, but any reasonable person would want to be a librarian."

She smiled again, but I could tell that she felt a little dismissed. "I actually do work with an archive, though."

"Do you?"

"I'm on the board of the Organization for Transformative Works." She fingered the edge of the cup and finally threw it away. "So we run something called the Archive of Our Own, which is for fan fiction—"

"Oh, I'm *very* familiar." I felt my voice drop three notes, the way people's voices do when they meet another person who's ever been deep in fandom. The vocal cords thicken with irony and the dirt of the trenches, and you don't have to say any more; you know you share a secret. She noticed that, and all at once her face was approachable and wry, each smile line clutching tight some small emotion.

"What fandoms?"

"Original *Trek*," I said, "*Lord of the Rings*, the movies. That's neat, though, that you work with the AO3."

"I'm really proud of it. People don't think fandom's important to remember."

"Well," I said, "they think it's ephemeral. But I have twenty feet of boxes labeled 'ephemera' in the back."

After the meeting I took out my phone and looked at my face in it. I can't see myself in a mirror, but I can see myself in a camera, and so I am used by now to seeing myself washed-out and grainy. My little face looked back at me, sallow with smooth delicate skin, my long-drawn teeth, the chin-length hair—brushed back—that I've never cut because I might regret it and my hair will never grow again. Was my chin a little squarer, my nose a little bigger? Everything seemed to be going so slowly. My eyes were hot in their sockets and when I closed them I saw bars of light. I needed my transfusion.

It was the end of November, and the sun went down at four thirty, but I waited until seven to go outside. You can't be too careful with the sun. In my building, there were three doors between the sky and the stairwell, but still, I caught myself paranoid that visitors would bring the sunlight in on their glowing skin, or that the elevator would slide open and release a cube of trapped sunlight to batter me to death against the wall. I smelled the sun in the fresh-air smells that caught and eddied on their coats, and in the cigarette smells that came down the vents from the street. It infused the greens I ate, it seemed caught in the reflection of my leather shoes, which had once been a cow's skin. But the archives were one of the safest places in the city, and I left them only in the full dark. Once, I'd had other things than the archives—a home, a car, ferry trips and hikes and cups of ice cream in a hot tanned hand—but these memories had dulled next to my terror of the annihilating light.

The transfusion clinic was kept dim, and only one unsavory fluorescent light burned above the three recliners. I took my place in the middle one, my least favorite. Two other vampires with whom I had a nodding acquaintance were seated in the other two chairs, having obviously been there for at least an hour. They looked sleepy, puffy-faced, that blood-drunk look. I closed my eyes too when they put the needle into the IV port in my chest, too tired to do anything but listen to the television. The IV and the TV. They used to call it the TV/TS split, transvestite or transsexual. If you'd put a glass to my mouth and held my nose, I don't believe I would have had the strength to swallow.

I felt better after the transfusion, my arms humming with fresh live blood. Blood lives only about a week inside me. I don't believe that anyone would give a damn about keeping vampires alive, except that they don't need to spend good blood on us— they don't even have to screen it, and they pull it out of anyone who comes in off the street to donate for the fee that my subscription supports. HIV, hep, all the blood-borne diseases: they die in me after two days. There's been research on this, trying to figure out what our bodies secrete that can kill anything, but so far no one understands it, and anyway all the studies are on a certain kind of vampire—male and turned within the past ten years. Technically, I fulfill both of those requirements, but I'm not the kind of male that interests the scientists. I've tried, but they tell me the XY chromosomes are what they care about, and the testosterone must be made in the same body that uses it.

I let myself back into the archives feeling sticky and lumpen, but better. Warmer. Someone just needed to whisk these congealing lumps of blood into a thinner paste. I did some exercises—yoga, push-ups, pull-ups—haphazardly and badly, which helped, and then I sat down and tried to read *Middlemarch*. But my concentration's not great right after the transfusion; I feel blurry, bloated, a little drunk. It takes the rest of the night to even out, and then I'm okay for a couple of days. Anyway, I put *Middlemarch* down, because the phone rang and I forgot that it wasn't daytime.

"Historical Society of Northern California. This is Sol Katz."

"I thought I'd get your voice mail," said Elsie. She had a

remarkable voice, a voice with more body in it than most, that used the whole of the throat. "Why are you at work?"

"Grant deadline." My heavy tone was artificial; I love writing grants.

"You must care more about your work than I ever have about anything. You could at least write it at home."

Sometimes at night, my office did feel like a home—the angle of the light was the same, but the silence, just me and the buglike rustling of the collections, turned it quiet and sour and safe. I didn't feel strange taking off my clothes. But tonight that feeling hadn't kicked in, or maybe I was still blood-drunk; I saw a warm halo around the transom window over my door.

"Do you want me to send you to voice mail?"

"Ah, no. Actually, I did want to talk to you. If your grant—"

"It's done. Now I'm busy making it worse." The phone receiver was cold against my face; I switched it to the other ear. "Help me get my mind off it. You're worried about the donation?"

"Yeah."

"How so?"

"How do people let *go* of these things?" Her voice was lightly suspended on a puff of breath. "Even if they want to. Even if I want to."

I put my feet up against the side of the bookcase by my desk, small insectile feet in black Converses with no dirt on the white soles. "It's hard. It's why people are always trying to give me their porn."

"What!"

"Our porn's alive," I said. "It's ours. It's *us*. We need to find a home for it. Isn't that what the AO3 is about?"

"Well, fanfic's about much more than porn—"

"Wasn't for me," I said, and she laughed.

"I wrote whole PG-rated novels. I was a big-name fan, you know. I was SylviaSalazar."

"Oh, God, *really*?"

I'd meant to sound impressed, but I'd despised that writer's work back in the nineties, and now it left me gasping with startled laughter. She was right; they'd been long, clean, polite stories, prose as dry and impactful as a dinosaur's footprint. Straight-A student fanfic, with no mess or sweat in it.

"It's how I met Tracy. She was teaching a class at the community college in Marin. And there I was, pleated skirt, patterned explicitly after Thora Birch in *Ghost World*, a very young twenty-five. I thought I could sashay up to her, cut her a little in multiple senses, show her I could do more with her characters than she could. You know that fan-writer arrogance."

"It's not arrogance," I said. "It's a good workman's pride in coming in at night and fixing the things the day workers broke. And it's a feminine pride—the only pride most men allow women to have, knowing that they've solved everyone's problems without being detected."

"It sounds like fanfic *was* a little more than porn to you."

"Nope. Anyway, I take it she didn't bow to you."

"No. She hated my work. And when I asked why, because I *was* a young twenty-five, she told me it was because she admired it and thought I was talented, but I'd let myself become a hack. Which was true. And I knew it was true. I'd never felt so seen." A tiny deliberate cough, like the period at the end of a sentence. "Have you ever had something very *beautiful* happen, but built on something that wasn't healthy at all? Because after that we fell in love. She loved me more than I loved her. I know that's true. Here I was, average-looking, average intelligence, an average writer, more than convinced that I was much more than average, that I had the world in a lozenge and all I had to do was pop it in my mouth, but here was this stately, powerful, *gorgeous* butch, and she came to need me like a machine needs a battery. And *I was a young twenty-five*."

"Was that a rhetorical question?"

"Which one?"

"Have I had something beautiful happen, built on something that wasn't healthy at all," I said. I was nervous, unaccountably nervous; my hand shook as it brushed the glossy coolness of my forehead.

"Have you?"

"No," I said. "My life hasn't been that messy. I don't think that's a good thing, but there you are. Anyway, this is pretty far afield of your question. And the porn example *was* part of that, by the way. There are a lot of ways to refuse to let something go."

"So what are you telling me? Not to refuse . . . ?"

"I'm telling you to let me worry about it instead," I said. "Let me launder your pain like Mob money. It's my literal job."

"Touché," she said, and I did feel it, through the phone, I felt the touch, the very palpable hit, my thin brittle saber against her jacketed chest. "I'm glad I met you. You're honest."

"Indifferent honest," I said. "But when I lie, they're unusual lies."

"It's hard for me to imagine you lying."

"I've lied twice in this conversation alone."

"Oh, yeah? Well, I could ask, but I won't." She coughed. "Good night, Sol. Good night, moon."

"Good night, Wedding-Guest and the loud bassoon."

When I'd hung up the phone I stared at it for a while. I didn't know where all that had come from, two lies and the Coleridge bit. It was like something from *Gatsby*: "That's the secret of Castle Rackrent." I didn't even know what the second lie had been.

And now that the conversation had been punctured and I was coming down, I felt the desire that had been in me. I'd loved listening to the tiny noises of her throat. On the phone everything is breath and speech; it is the least articulate medium for talking to people, the one with the least information, and yet the most intimate one. It's on the phone and during sex that we notice breath the most. Now I could barely catch mine, empty reflex though it was.

I'm always a little terrified by desire. For so many years I did not know what to do with it; the bubble of heat embarrassed me at best, panicked me at worst. How do you feel desire with a body that you can't bear to have touched? Transition was just beginning to change that when I became a vampire—a state in which I had hardly been touched by desire at all. The blood ran down through the cold, ridged gutters of my body, disinterested in flowing anywhere specific.

Of course, the stereotype of vampires is the opposite: that we are sexually insatiable, and that when we get to fucking, we have trouble controlling our urge to sink our teeth into people's necks. What I've found is that both are slightly true, though for other reasons than you'd think. The insatiability, both kinds, comes from loneliness and fear, and the relief of being held although we are cold. We want to be held so much that we sometimes consent to be held by people we *know* are playing Russian roulette with our bodies—who are drawn to that chance of a bite, and the little chance within that bigger chance of becoming something like me, something that can be scorched to death by the touch of daylight.

But I was afraid. The phone had been the only thing that protected me from wanting, and it was a very thin thing, a bit of plastic, a rubber cord. I had never failed in my defenses before. I'd never been in love either, except with television.

There's so little to do at night in the city, especially after the bars close. The only things that stay open twenty-four hours are a few restaurants and the gyms and drugstores. I've killed time at all three, but it always died hard. Tonight I went out to a Walgreens a mile away, a safe distance to walk in winter. I felt shaky and blue although I was hot and red with blood. I hadn't felt this physically weak in years. I rarely go outside after three a.m., even in winter with three whole glassy hours hanging from the tree until dawn, but I was too restless.

The office was on the border of the Financial District and the Tenderloin. In front of the tech company headquarters, there was life: men selling sunglasses, clothes, and household supplies off lumpy blankets. Not far off was Folsom and its leather bars. Uptown, there were some places that also stayed open quite late, a few coffee shops and the lobbies of the great hotels.

At the drugstore, I pretended to look at soda and herbal nonsense, just to have something to do, a different kind of fluorescent light crawling over me. I barely knew how to use the city then. Now I do.

CHAPTER 2

Feet of Clay

When I was young and watched TV for sustenance instead of pleasure, I watched nothing more often than *Feet of Clay*, which Elsie's wife, Tracy, had created. It had hit me in the tenderest part of my adolescence, the sharp hinge under the skin of 1993, a funny bone far too delicate to absorb any real blows. Not that I was ever really an adolescent, but I had the tenderness of one. That's what it's like to be a trans child and not know it. You have all the fragility of adolescence, but none of its resilience, the clever cartilage that always grows back.

The X-Files was a few years old then, but everyone was still talking about aliens and conspiracies. I remember that time, with its faint stink of documentary, when there was a secret under every sodden and mildewed thing you picked up in the woods. People seemed to assume *The X-Files* was a dramatization of something real. *Feet of Clay* was a knockoff, really, except set in space, but as often happens with knockoffs, this one secured something genuinely creepy. A doppelgänger of the real show. The actors were an uncanny valley version of Duchovny's and Anderson's already uncanny faces. (His bonier than it's supposed to be, and somehow overgrown; hers with no more detail than the moon.) Instead of those two, *Feet of Clay* had Randall M. Groves and Joshua Stack and Ella du Bois and Ali Payne: Groves with his blocky head and the air that it burdened him, Stack with his vampish mathematical perfection and long chin, du Bois a spider caught in her own gray web, and Payne as butch as women on TV then could dare be.

At the beginning, the explorers played by du Bois and Payne discovered a group of shape-shifting aliens—ostensibly made of clay, though they always looked like what they were: actors draped in layers of drippy Technicolor latex. They were called the miha. Once they arrived on human planets, they began killing people, replacing them, and taking over their lives as if nothing had happened, and killing in turn anyone who seemed to notice or complain. By the end of the show, most of the extras you saw in the background were miha, and most of the main characters were adept at pretending they hadn't noticed.

It was a time when telling your stories in arcs was still new, and most shows compromised on a pattern of artfully scattered monster-of-the-week episodes combined with arcs that kicked in for the true faithful. *Feet of Clay* was different. It was more of an anthology of life with the miha: police cases,

were all mine. At night, Shalk sits around in his underpants and watches Zaduk on CCTV as he reads or sleeps or fucks. I understood Shalk more than anything, and I obsessed about his body without knowing why—his pale hairy thighs, his loose throat, his good arms. It soothed me to think of that body piled around mine as I tried to sleep. It was a guilty secret, a shameful secret, and for years I could not talk about these characters without blushing.

At home, after buying a couple of bottles of juice at Walgreens and carefully putting them on the table the archives designates for drinks with covers, I sat down to watch an episode of the show. It had been so long that I just picked my favorite, which tracks sixteen hours in the lives of Zaduk and Shalk.

Zaduk is breaking up with a woman he's been seeing for a few episodes, and he argues with her in a café. Shalk's tension is going up, his instincts are kicking in, he plays a tape of a former Zaduk killing a lover, and the lines, the moves are the same— Zaduk repeats them, tape-Zaduk repeats them, and Shalk shouts the same lines over them both. The argument ends, though, with no violence. Shalk sits back in shock. Zaduk leaves, goes to a bar, gets drunk, picks a fight, and Shalk spools up again, but of course Zaduk doesn't know how to fight. He is beaten violently and left for dead. Shalk, who has only been watching him all day, forgetting to eat and care for himself, leaps up, runs to the scene, and finds Zaduk still there, lying on the sidewalk in the dark. Zaduk asks, "How did you get here so fast?" Shalk says, "I was watching you on CCTV." Zaduk says, "Why?" Shalk says, "Because the city loves you and wants you to be safe." Zaduk passes out from the pain then, and they don't speak of it again. Credits. *Created by Trace Britton.*

Why did she use that form of her name, so obviously intended to be ambiguous? Trace, a leftover pencil mark. I'd felt an obscure thrill when I learned that Trace was a woman. For some people, it seemed very easy to get inside a male identity and steer it with two careful hands. I knew I could never do anything like that.

After the episode was over, I just sat in the dark. The thing was that the episode still had me. You'd expect an old fandom like that, whose purpose was spent, would spill from my mouth like ashes, but it didn't. Watching those men look at each other, I felt the same longing and fear as I had at fifteen, when my whole life was longing and fear. The difference between me and most teenagers was that I didn't know what I longed for, and I sure didn't know what I was afraid of.

CHAPTER 3

A Butch

The boxes came in, all one hundred of them, via two-day FedEx from the North Bay. File boxes and old moving boxes; Amazon boxes large and small. One was a wooden file cabinet. Attached to these was a rainbow of tape: packing, masking, electrician's, and Scotch.

I feigned a migraine to avoid going up to the loading dock. Nobody ever caught on that I always had a migraine on unloading day. I remembered to feign migraines on other days too. It took up all my time to remember who I was supposed to be, this character I overlaid on myself to pretend my life was normal.

Toward the end of the afternoon, when all the boxes had been staged in the hallway, I feigned a lifting of the migraine and volunteered to move them. Although it had been less than a day since my last transfusion, I really did feel somewhat weak; my bones felt splintered, dry in my body. Perhaps it was an ill person's blood again that ran, cooling and sloppy, in the dark channels of me. Sometimes I get a touch of that person's body in mine, like a hand in a hand, like a song playing in another room and scenting the air of yours. It's always only a touch. I couldn't tell you what made them ill, or what their personalities were like. Once in a while, the clinic had fucked up and given me women's blood, which of course carries estrogen instead of testosterone—I still take a T shot, but only to augment the blood. I knew the estrogen had come because I felt a little smaller and less firm in my skin, and slippery, and weepy.

"Are you really feeling better, Sol?" Florence asked, as we were hefting boxes side by side. Florence was the assistant archivist, a dyke in her fifties, powdered with archival dust, glowing with health, and oozing sympathy. She had a way of asking if I was feeling better—skeptically, as if I might be lying about it—that made it clear she thought I was lying about having been sick in the first place. Didn't mean I didn't pretend well, or that she was observant. Florence was just like that.

"Oh, I'm good," I said. "Thank you for handling the loading dock."

"It's what you asked me to do," she said resignedly. "What do you think of all the tape?"

"What about it?"

"Well," she said, and dropped a box onto another. "I think it's deranged."

"She just wanted to get it over with," I said. "It was the middle of the night. She ran out of supplies and started to improvise, and pretty soon she started feeling like a genius."

"How do you know?"

"I know how people think in the middle of the night," I said. Tired, in distress, just wanting it to be over: I've glued original art to cardboard because it had been sitting unframed for months, and have hemmed T-shirts with scissors and watched in dismay as they became belly shirts. What we do when we can't wait anymore, and the waiting has caused such distress, such static electricity in the limbs, sand in the blood and sandpaper in the joints, that we act without control and without sense.

I could see Elsie, controlled though she had been when we met, tearing through her kitchen drawers looking for more tape, her face awful and focused. I watched the nape of her neck, the muscles tense, her smooth hands locating what she was looking for. Sweatpants, a T-shirt with that perfect point of stress over her tits. The thought made the pressure change in my body, the barometer shift. I stopped, adjusted my grip on the box, unbalanced.

"I think she's nuts," said Florence, bringing me back to the moment. I looked at her over the boxes. Florence is cool, in the way that only older lesbians can be cool. Strong forearms, pinkie ring, flinty look. I always want to be bitchy with her, to sequester ourselves for a moment in a cone of breath and tell each other who's sane and who's nuts, but the trouble is that she's too sane and I'm too nuts. And I don't mean that to indict myself. I mean that to indict her.

Florence once saw a pre-transition photo of me on Facebook and told me that I look exactly the same as I did. She's shown me pictures of her wife, talked about how she used to hate being a woman, just like I did, but her wife showed her how to love it, and it saved her life. She's sent me an article about the dangers of chest binding. I couldn't with her, I tell you.

"She's grieving, Florence."

"Have you seen the ones I opened?"

"Not yet," I said. "Are they in the reading room?"

"Yeah, hold on. Take five. Let me show you." She motioned me back through the archives and into the reading room, with its conference table and red chairs. On the table were several boxes slit open carefully with Florence's mother-of-pearl pocket-knife. I peeked into one and saw that the files were splattered with something clear and brown.

"Dr Pepper, I thought," said Florence, "but maybe Diet Coke. She does seem like the Diet Coke type."

I gave the box a sniff, smelled nothing but musty garage. No mold, no aspartame. Pulling up one of the files inside, I gave a start—it was full of liquid and nothing else. The other files held sheafs of paper, and I rapidly lifted them out to save them from the splash.

"Florence, did you pull this one out already? Is that why the stuff's all over?"

"Yeah, but I didn't fill it with *soda*, Sol."

"It's not soda. It's like—like sap. And there's no way it was in here when she shipped it. The truck would have bounced the goo all over the box."

"You just like her," said Florence. "And this is what I'm always saying about how you're too trusting."

"The sap would have been everywhere. It's physics."

"She cried in your office for five minutes. The warbling got five times louder when you opened the door to get her water, which, by the way, I guess the liquid rule doesn't matter for her—"

"Tears are liquids too," I said. "You can't keep *everything* out of the archives."

"It's more like you can't keep *anything* out of them," said Florence, flicking pointedly at the label of the sap-filled folder: *Black Kite* Notes, 2017. "I've had it. I'm going on break."

That night I went to the gym upstairs for a shower. I had a card, stolen from one of the construction workers who were continually working on one of our building's floors. It let me into any of the levels, and could even freeze the elevator wherever it was, presumably so that they could reserve it to move their carts of fragments and dust.

I don't usually need a shower—my body produces sweat very slowly, the same way it does everything else, and when it comes, it's thick, concentrated, and a grit appears in my mouth. Vampirism stops the body, freezes it hard and cracks it beyond repair. I'm like a moldy attic, or a house with asbestos in the drywall; I still mostly work, but there are hazards to negotiate. When I first got sick, or rather was *made* sick, they made me walk up and down the halls of the hospital at night to stop my blood from pooling. The brownish light, the sheen of the walls, approached and receded. I felt a new kind of tiredness. My joints crackled, my hair coarsened, and the skin of my face grew dry through its whole thickness, like a dehydrated fruit. I cursed my work, for it had been there that the accident happened. Archives are full of poisons, but I never expected to die of them.

All this happened about a year into my transition, which had previously been a time of acceleration and glee. Since then, though I've kept up with my HRT and insisted on receiving only men's blood despite a surprising amount of medical resistance, transition has progressed like a drip of honey sliding down a jar: unctuous and slow, something sweet becoming dusty, dirty. I still saw a little fresh hair from time to time, or glanced at my face in my phone camera and felt that it had coalesced a little more, hardened, out of the early-T puffiness. And, of course, I still felt better than I had before, when there had seemed to be a half inch of air or a crackling substance between me and my skin, and a sense that if I moved too quickly, the muscle might touch the skin and it would be awful.

But I dissociated like hell during this shower. I flowed down my own body and down the drain with the hot water, and when it was done I combed my hair back with businesslike strokes of my fingers. This gym was attached to a tech company; the machines were all white and had parts that glowed a little. The showers were in little individual rooms, and there was a rack of towels kept warmed even at night. Going upstairs was like watching a TV show shift scenes, Captain Kirk beaming down to a new planet, even though you knew it was all shot on a soundstage next door.

When I got back to my office, in my sweatpants and the packer I sometimes wear at night for a little subversive relief, the voice mail light was blinking red. It was Elsie's number and I called it back without listening to the message.

"Your phone voice is so different from your voice in person." Elsie, like a character on television, never said hello.

"Is it?"

"Yes, it's much more confident."

"I don't always do well in person. Classic archivist."

She cleared her throat. "Well, that makes this next thing sound odd. Can I see you again? On a date? Unless you have some kind of professional rule against fraternizing with people like me."

"I do, but I already broke it." A rush, a puff of cold abrasive air, came into my head as at the opening of a valve. "I could fraternize with you, Elsie."

"A little twincest?"

"Oh, God, that's a deep cut. And a very painful one."

"You don't like *Supernatural*?"

"Can't stand it."

"Nor me."

"Good."

"Well, I'm glad," she said. "You're exactly my type. A cute, gallant butch. *Supernatural* would have broken the deal."

"Well," I said, "I'm not a butch."

"Oh, that's what all the butches say, Sol. What is it? You like a floral shirt? You can only fix an *electric* car?"

"Nobody can fix an electric car. They're total black boxes, if the battery breaks down you just need to replace the unit. But I'm—seriously, Elsie—I'm a trans man. I'm not a woman."

"Oh," said Elsie. "No, that's very obvious. I mean, that you're not a woman."

"Then you meant a butch man? Because I'm not that either."

"I thought you were one of those nonbinary people," she said cautiously. "There are so many of them now."

"Well—I'm not. I'm a man. I just don't pass."

"That doesn't matter to me."

"Possibly it should."

"I'm sorry. What did I say?"

"Nothing," I said. "Forget it. I'm too sensitive. A lesbian asks me out—"

"Oh, I'm very bi."

"Oh."

"I think you're really gorgeous," she said gently. "You're a hot butch—no matter what your gender—you're clear and steady and you have eyes like gems and veins like cloudy gems, and slim hands which are slicker and smoother than most people's hands. You're *hot*. I want to watch you write things on folders in small neat handwriting. I don't really care what you are, you're the kind of person I think is attractive, and I know I'm the kind of person *you* think is attractive. And I wanna have dinner and I don't wanna argue about it."

"What kind of gems?"

"Fuck you, I don't know. Emeralds. Sapphires."

"My eyes are brown."

"Topaz. I came out of nineties fanfic. Will you come out with me?"

"I'll drop you an email," I said. "And I'm not *a* butch."

CHAPTER 4

Series 1: Screenplays

INT, archives. Morning. SOL KATZ, 41, a youthful archivist with a pronounced lisp and chin-length hair pomaded and combed loosely back in a greasy dirtbag bob in the manner of Clea DuVall in *But I'm a Cheerleader* — a film which strongly influenced his lesbian coming-of-age, which never really got anywhere, due to later-to-be-realized "his" — cranks open a box cutter and breaks the seal of heavy tape on a LARGE BANKER'S BOX. CLOSE ON HIS FACE as he regards what's inside: sweaty, exhausted, with a painful swelling under the eyelids that speaks of a bad night. SOL never has a bad night, as he is a vampire and sleeps only occasionally, but somehow he has managed to be ill-rested anyway.

REVERSE SHOT: the inside of the box. Hanging files detached from their hangers, the metal ripped out with someone's hands. Rows and rows of material bound in plastic, whose scent and viscosity we can detect from the series of QUICK CUTS of Sol drawing his face closed and snapping on blue nitrile gloves. He's older than he looks, Sol, and we see it now: the wrinkles of his face, as it pantomimes weary disgust, are practiced wrinkles; they fall into predictable channels. He pulls out files and begins to read them. We see the pages illuminated, dense and greasy paper, by the lights that shine over his head. Typed with a typewriter, some handwritten, wads of cottony paper. PAGE AFTER PAGE flashes by, CUT AFTER CUT. Some of the folders are splattered with a viscous liquid, and these he replaces with new ones. He's not taking breaks, and we don't see anyone else in the shots as he sits at a cheap conference table covered in eraser shavings, rusted paper clips, and two yellow legal pads. Somehow we get the impression that Sol is smoking, although he is not. There's that same sense of brooding over something, hooded eyes and a light source that renews itself jankily, unpredictably, that same jittery sense of something boring but calming. MEDIUM SHOT as Sol slaps a folder full of material onto the table. He leans back, hitches at his belt. Sol has wide hips and a flat but generous ass whose two halves seem formed of specially made materials that would normally be part of a car. Leatherette and hard stuffing. They're designed for one purpose and one purpose only: to make men's pants fit badly. Sol is depressed now.

The camera follows FLORENCE, gray buzz cut and flannel shirt perfectly faded and pilled, into the conference room. Florence is grizzled and handsome; she stands out in any room like Porthos next to D'Artagnan, like a gold-swagged musketeer next to a recruit just dug out from the farm. This may explain why Sol hired her. It doesn't, however, at all explain why Sol drops his file like he's doing something wrong with it. He can hardly resist a snarl, a real snarl, like a dog. Florence sits down across from him and they look at each other from opposite sides of the frame.

Sol and Florence are the kind of enemies who almost like each other. Neither of them wants to hate the other, though they both blame Sol for the fact that they do. Nonetheless, under the banter, which comes easily, there's a seething quality, a sense that they are speaking quickly and lightly to stop any word from sinking in too deep.

FLORENCE

It's in bad shape, huh?

SOL

Horrible. You know how when you're at the beginning of processing, nothing looks good? Like, nothing looks like it can possibly be good, or ever will. I wanted this collection, I'm thrilled to be working with it, but it's a shit show. No original order whatsoever.

FLORENCE

Original chaos?

SOL

(Wearily. This is a standard archival joke.)

Chaos gives it too much credit. There was
chaos on the earth before God divided the
land from the waters. It's a noble calling,
being chaotic; it's one-third, or
realistically two-thirds, of all D&D
characters. This just isn't organized at all.
It is the work of a profoundly depressed
person. And I'm always tempted, if I'm
totally honest, to let it be that way. I know
it doesn't do anything for the researchers,
but there's this sentimental side of me that
just says — here — this came to me a mess
and I'll give it to you as a mess. I don't
want to organize it at all. This is a rich,
hoardy, information-bearing mess. This is a
primordial mess. This is the shape of a
person's mind, that carved pink eraser of
the brain. This will tell you everything you
need to know.

(It bears mentioning, here, that Sol sounds
a little like Steve Buscemi. When you're
doing transmasculine voice training, or at
least reading about voice training on the
Internet, you're encouraged to record
yourself and to try and think of a man you
want to emulate, a man you'd like to sound

like, to fuck-or-be. For Sol, whose rich
crackling shaken-sheet-of-metal voice is
the one part of him that makes people
automatically call him "sir," this was
Buscemi, whose nasal rasp sounds like a
perfect game of pool. It's not just the
working-class imagery — to which Sol as a
child of moderate privilege should really
not aspire — nor the superb control the
man has, but the simple, cool thunk of the
ball that makes Sol associate that sound
with billiards. Sol rarely goes to bars,
though he goes to more of them now that
the sun will kill him. But he does love
the sound of pool, and he loves the sound
of Steve Buscemi, and years ago in earnest
desperation he spent a lot of time trying
to manage those tones, with the result
that the grind of testosterone has
produced something rich as coffee in his
throat.)

                    FLORENCE

I mean, it has information, but not
interesting information.

                      SOL

I know. I'm just saying that sticking to
original order, which is all about
pretending we're neutral, is also kind of
aesthetically fun.

FLORENCE

What are you going to do?

SOL

The series are screenplays, show bibles,
subject files — lots of those, I'm sorry to
say — personal correspondence, business
correspondence —

FLORENCE

Jesus, it's got more series than Italian
soccer.

SOL

Doesn't that just mean it has more than two?

FLORENCE

Technically, it's nine. Serie A, Serie B,
Serie C, Serie D, Excellence, Promotion,
First Category, Second Category, and Third
Category.

      (With laborious bonhomie.)
Hey, tag yourself.

SOL

Third Category.

FLORENCE

Well, there's no need to be self-deprecating.

SOL

Is that the bad end of the scale?

FLORENCE

Yes.

SOL

I've always been told I'm kind of a third
category.

FLORENCE

Well, you're sure taking a while to get from
A to B.

SOL

What about you?

FLORENCE

(Relaxed.)

Serie B? I've always felt like I'm a
professional-level player, but not the kind
that really makes it — like if I were an
athlete, David Foster Wallace would profile
me, or rather he would think about it and
then not.

SOL

(Absently, and touching the cold skin
of his arm.)

"Both flesh and not."

(He comes back to himself.)

Anyway, those are the series. There might be
one or two more, depending on how I chop up
the correspondence. But I don't think people
will come here for her business letters,
anyway, and it all feels too fussy. Sorry to
be a piss.

FLORENCE

(An edge here. She *knows* Sol's annoyed by
being advised without permission. She might
also be fishing for something else.)

Honestly, Sol? You should get outside more.
The files will still be here if you go take
a walk. It's really nice out.

SOL

I might later.

FLORENCE

(Hearty.)

No, I'm sorry, I'm fucking with you. The rain
hasn't stopped.

SOL

Oh. It's okay.

CHAPTER 5

The Milwaukee Protocol

I was napping in my office when the phone rang, and this time I had the sense, even in the gelatinous half sleep of five p.m. on a Saturday, not to pick it up. I was lying under the electric blanket, a long habit of mine—although the heat didn't really get into me, it was comforting to feel it against the fuzzy skin. A book and my laptop, with its endless fan of movies, were at my side. Silence. Brief drooping of lids.

The phone rang again, the second bank of rings coming right on top of the first, like two rows disappearing in *Tetris*. I got up, scattering my things, saw Elsie's number, and picked up.

"I'm here," she said, and her voice was warped and weak. "Can you come up and get me?"

"What's happened?"

"Nothing. I just hate driving, and—I had a bad night last night. I know I'm really early. I wasn't sure I'd catch you. Sol—are you okay?"

"Why would I not be?"

"Don't patronize me. Why are you never not at work? Why didn't you give me your cell number?"

"Look," I said. "No. I—I'm going to send you up a card."

"What?"

"I can't come up. I'm sorry. It's a long story. I don't get cell reception down here anyway—"

"Are you on the run from the law?" Her voice was a little calmer now.

"No. You need to go to the elevator on the far left—I'll put my keycard in it—to get down to the basement. I'll send it up to you. You come down to me."

"Are you sick?"

"No more than usual," I said, a half-truth for which I despised myself as the receiver went down, but sometimes we can't tell the whole one without the half first, like titration.

Illness wasn't the right word for my vampirism—I saw vampirism as something that fundamentally disqualified me from life, that limited me to a half-life or a third-life, depending on the time of the year—and I knew that calling myself sick made me too sympathetic. Perhaps it even suggested I was dying, while in fact by any medical measure I was already dead. But there I was, three hours before the time set for our date, which was supposed to be the comfortable, chilly after-hours time of seven p.m.—jamming the DOOR OPEN button on the elevator, conscious of dear Elsie shifting her weight and looking down at her expensive shoes fifteen feet above me. I leaned my head against the wall for a moment and thought of her presence moving toward me.

God, she was exactly my type too—which is to say the kind of person *I'd* been in the nineties. Goth when I could afford it, owner of too many garments that laced up, hair gone bronze or gold or metallic purple with overdyeing, nose ring like a little magnet, home-sewn costuming of upholstery fabric, cheap velvet, cheap chenille, expensive tastes on no budget until you have a budget, and then the same tastes, baked in. I knew the person who was about to come out of that elevator, and we were about to find out just how afraid of that I was.

She embraced me as soon as she stepped through the doors. I was surprised to realize that she was much taller than me, and that there was sun and wind caught in the wiry black snares of her coat. I felt her supporting herself on me, just a bit, the way muscle is supported by bone. Then we parted, and I kept my hands on her waist for a moment.

"Are you okay?" I asked her, partly to stop her from asking if I was.

"I'm scared of driving on these highways," she said. "I make myself do it, but it's getting worse. Last night I barely even slept, knowing I'd have to drive at night. I almost canceled. But finally it got to be too late, I knew it was too late to cancel. But, Sol—are *you* all right? You said something about being sick."

"Not seriously," I said. "Come and have a cup of tea. I'm, uh—I'm scared of driving too. I sold my car years ago." I didn't mention that it was because cars are mostly windows.

I took her to the break room: gingham tablecloth, plastic scrims of blue skies over the fluorescent lights. The electric kettle made its settled little sounds. I sensed Elsie calming down just slightly, and then Florence came in.

"Hey," she said, in a dead voice.

"Hey," I said, and half rose, as if to greet a visiting dignitary. "I didn't know you were coming in. Elsie, this is Florence—the assistant archivist here."

"Hi," said Elsie, with a tired smile.

"Sol," said Florence, "what's this about?"

"I am here on a Saturday," I said, "doing some work, and my date came over a little early. Why do you ask?"

There was a peculiar tight energy about Florence. I mistook it for the tension of a person who expected to be alone; now I realize that it was the tension of a chess player who sees a mate in five, but is not quite confident enough to announce it. The tension of someone who knows that they need to manage this carefully. All nerves, no breath.

"Why did you let your date"—here Florence nodded to Elsie, as if to say: *This is you*—"come over early?"

"Sometimes dates do that," I said. "It's not unknown. Florence, what is this about?"

"I just asked you the same thing, and then you pointed out that I'm just your assistant."

"You're not—it was the other way around, wasn't it?"

"Nope," said Florence, and now she was swinging. "You're bringing people here for sex. Why?"

"I'm not," I said. "Where are you getting this? I'm—"

"There's wet washcloths on the floor of your office. There's clothes. There's a dildo."

"I don't *own*—"

"I literally saw it five minutes ago. Are you telling me I don't know what a dick looks like? I was married to a man for fifteen years."

"The packer," I said. "I do have a packer. I'm—I'm sorry you saw that—"

The kettle, which had been boiling, clicked off. Elsie said, "Do the two of you want to step it down for a second?"

"Why would I want to do that?" asked Florence politely.

"Let me put it this way. What do you want to come out of this?" Elsie looked—not calm, not resolute, as tense as either of us, but nonetheless there was a firmness about her. "What do you expect to get out of it?"

"What are you implying?"

"I'm saying that if you're unhappy with the way Sol keeps his office, or you think something inappropriate is going on, you should go to HR about it. Right now your only audience is Sol, who you're accusing, and me, who's going to defend him. You need to think strategically, if you're making a complaint."

"Maybe I will," said Florence icily. "Thank you for your advice."

"You are wrong, though," said Elsie, "about the office. Or you're wrong about me. I just got here. That's why I have my coat on."

"Oh, yes," said Florence, "you're a *great* detective."

"You have no idea who I am."

"You're Tracy Britton's wife."

"I was her wife, yes."

"I'm going to go," said Florence. "You're right, Mrs. Britton, this isn't going anywhere."

"Oh, please," said Elsie, but Florence, making a sort of time-out gesture with a flat tight mouth, was already on her way out the door. We stood there and listened until the elevator dinged.

"I was going to say, 'Oh, please, Mrs. Britton is my dead wife's homophobic mother,'" said Elsie. "So perhaps it's just as well."

"Thank you."

"For what?"

"For helping."

"Oh, no, I think I made it worse. What is her deal?"

"She's . . ." I got up and paced the room. "Um, I think she just hates me."

"She's your assistant?"

"She's *the* assistant. Not mine specifically. I hired her a few years ago—I was the one who really wanted to hire her. Nobody else liked her as much as me. But she really hates me, and I think it's partly for good reasons."

"Which are?"

Words were cascading out of me now, hyperkinetic and hypermobile. "I'm a *terrible* boss. They keep promoting me, is the problem. Because I'm so good at entry-level archives shit, but it turns out I'm bad at administration. So to replace me, because I'm bad at administration, I hired someone who's no good at entry-level archives shit and just grandstands around the office all day. And she knows I know."

"Well, if you see what's wrong, you can fix what's wrong."

"I can't."

"Why?"

"She doesn't like that I'm trans," I said, aware of how weak it sounded. "Been pretty open about it."

"Was it stupid of me to tell her to go to HR?"

"No. They're okay. I should have gone to them about *her*. A long time ago. The thing is that I didn't expect it—I always assume that when she says things, she must mean them innocently. I think I'm a pretty innocuous person—maybe it's all a front, I guess, a way to be cute and harmless and abdicate responsibility for all my sins—"

"Sol," said Elsie.

"Yeah?"

"What has she *said* to you?"

I told her about the articles, the discourses on her wife, but I added, "But she's right. I mean, she's wrong, but she's right. I stay in my office every night. It's the only way to be safe from the evening and the morning."

There was a shiver of reaction in her face, a faint sigh, as if to say, *I sure can pick 'em.* But all she said was, "What do you mean?"

"I'm a vampire."

The words slipped out easily, easily as a tongue between lips. I'd rehearsed those words a thousand times, said them perhaps five. My boss and HR knew, and my mother, but as for telling my friends—I'd lost them, even the oldest of them, rather than do that. It wasn't that I was ashamed. It's that I was dead, and when you're dead, nothing on that side of the river means much to you anymore. My friends had turned to sunlight; they had vaporized, and I stayed underground, where dead people belong.

But when I said it to Elsie, it was just a fact. And her shock, though it came, was a sympathetic shock, two bodies vibrating at the same frequency.

"You *are*?"

"I got too afraid to be anywhere but here," I said, my voice cracking open. "When this first happened to me, I once spent a whole day in a bathroom—the single-person kind—with wads of toilet paper stuffed under the door. Someone who worked in the coffee shop finally figured out someone had been in there since dawn and we had a shouting fight through the door. I had to yell that I was a fucking vampire through the door at everybody."

"Jesus, Sol. I'm sorry." She was smoothing, smearing, at my hair.

"I'm used to it."

"A vampire. Jesus." She pressed her palms to the side of my head and stared into my face for a long moment. "I know you're not as young as you look, but sometimes you look twenty-two to me."

"A young twenty-two?"

"A very tired one." She pulled my face to her shoulder. "And one who needs to stop talking now."

"I'm sorry."

"I like you because you're a talker. I can't fault you for it. But you're making me feel like your mom."

"Oh," I said, lifting my face away. "Oh, God, why don't I just stop doing that?"

She touched my shoulder, then pulled away, going to the kettle, pouring hot water into cups. "Let's go sit in your office, yeah? We can sit on the couch where you'll feel safer. I bet it's nice; there's even a dildo."

"Oh, you can't bring drinks in there."

Elsie glittered her eyes at me. "Are you kidding? You just copped to sleeping in your office, and I can't bring my drink into the archives? I even had one before."

"There are some rules that matter and some that don't matter."

"Sol." She bent back over me, her hands tight around the muscles of my upper arms. It made me feel both strong and weak, full of power and exhausted. I closed my eyes and felt her mouth on my mouth, cool and slick with red lipstick, going on easily. Just a faint brush of a kiss like a brush of paint.

"You're beautiful," I said automatically.

"Come. Come." She led me into the archives proper and I steered us into the office, kicking the packer under the desk on the way in.

I sat her down on my black leather couch, which is a very unsexy—neutering, really—thing to make out of black leather. Like a deflated animal, that couch; I inherited it from the previous occupant. Then I realized that she had never taken her black fleece coat off. I offered to take it, and she undid the buttons and arched her body up so that it fell away from her, but didn't go any further. Her eyes went glassy, inert, like a sleeping computer, and suddenly I felt very fond of her. I said, "You're really afraid of driving, huh?"

"She used to do all the driving," said Elsie, and rolled her head a little on the back of the couch. "I know everything I say about her is like a cliché. Nobody wants to be a cliché. Nobody wants to be boring. But I can't ever get her out of me."

"You sound like it was miserable."

"On the contrary," she said wretchedly. "It was great. The trouble is that I can't remember the great parts. Sol, don't talk about me. There's nothing interesting about me."

"I used to think I wasn't interesting."

"What changed?"

"I transitioned. Turned out I was interesting, I just didn't want to look at myself."

"Oh." She made a fretful sound. "Hah—well, I don't think

that's in the cards for me. Look at this." She gestured at her lush and mutable body, her wrap dress with the pattern of chevrons, the cleavage almost comically decorated with a little chevron necklace.

"That's what I thought too, though. I didn't think my body could change that much, until it did."

"Well, you're different, you're—flat," she said, as if the adjective had had to drop a long way toward her. "I mean, you have a very boyish body."

"I really didn't used to. And I still have this ass."

"I know," she said. "Come sit by me, you're making me nervous." I sat, and she said, "You're still making me nervous."

"You need me to sit differently?" I had my knees up on the sofa, my legs tucked under me; it's how I always sit. She reached out and touched my knee. Her touch was again almost as cold as mine, and I had the impression she was reaching out for comfort as much as to comfort me, as if my knee were a life jacket floating on water.

"You're freezing."

"Yes."

"Do you feel it?"

"No."

"How did it happen?"

"They do it with a blood transfusion," I said.

"On purpose? Who's 'they'?"

"Well," I said, "it's a weird disease. People used to get it through rat bites—from infected rats. When they didn't get it from other vampires, of course. Most bites don't infect people, but nobody knows why, and nobody really knows what controls it. It's dangerous in other ways. You can die of infections from having a person's teeth bite into you. Um, it's messy. I don't like it very much. My body temperature is in the sixties. My heart and my lungs don't have to work. My fucking testosterone barely works anymore—trans people who meet me think I just started transitioning. I feel disgusting. I'm amazed that you weren't disgusted by kissing me. Isn't it like kissing a dead person?"

"I couldn't be disgusted by you. Kissing your mouth was like—slipping into a pool in hot weather. When you're very hot, and you need to cool off or you feel like you'll die. And your mouth is soft—cool and soft—like milk."

"Oh," I said. She slipped her arm around me, with an apologetic, supplicating look, and put her other hand on my belly. I fell apart into her then, my head against her shoulder. The part of me that's always a little outside my body started bleating its little questions: *Am I sleepy? Am I turned on? Am I relaxed?* And then it hushed, because I was in a state of awareness of *her* body, which slipped into me suddenly, as if I had fallen a short way. The heat radiating off of her was like a hot sidewalk with light dancing on it. I wanted that light for my own.

"Tell me how it happened," she said again.

"Tetanus."

"Tetanus?"

My face doesn't redden anymore, and when I would normally have blushed, I just felt a density to the cold, like a fusion of cloudy glass. A greater solidity in a face that normally felt like water; a sudden freeze that cracked my cheeks. I rubbed my face between my thumb and forefinger. "I almost died of tetanus and they gave me this to keep me alive."

"I've never heard of that."

"Most people haven't. If you've ever heard of the Milwaukee Protocol for rabies—"

"No."

"You put the person in a coma and give them antiviral drugs." I was talking as much as I could in order to avoid the simple pull of her body. "The idea is that since the disease uses the body's own strength and activity against it, minimizing activity in the brain keeps the damage limited—so you have a chance to build up antibodies before the disease kills you. It doesn't work, is the problem. The first person they tried it on did live, but she was an outlier for a couple of different reasons. But it gave a doctor in Washington State—Meta Dinius—the idea to treat tetanus a different way. I don't understand at all how it works."

"Go on," she said. She had brown eyes, and their corners were the softest pink, a softness that wasn't like a wet eye at all but like fur, a rabbit, a bunny.

"I reached into this coffee can of pinback buttons," I said. "They were YES ON 19 buttons, 2010. It was a failed pot legalization law. The can was full of rust, and so were the button backs, and I don't know how it happens—archival stuff just twists its way into your flesh sometimes, dried-up old rubber band bits, God knows what—but one of these pins just went straight under my nail and deep into my finger."

"Ow! Ow, fuck, God."

"Exactly. That's what I said. I went to urgent care—every bump of the car agony, of course, because I didn't dare pull it out, and the tip of the pin was biting into me where I was already hurt—"

"Ow." She was actually crying a little, her eyes welling pinker and pinker. I shifted on the sofa, put my feet on the floor. Suddenly I felt a buildup, a prick, of twitchy energy.

"Well, it wasn't *that* bad."

"It sounds agonizing, and you died."

I watched my hand, veiny and small, sitting on my knee. I was still in my sweatpants and the inside-out T-shirt I wear when I lie down. No wonder Florence had caught on right away.

"You have to understand, this is just my life now." I was swimming out of my body a little. "I need to go outside."

"Can we?" She glanced at her phone; the weather app showed the moon. I said, "In a half hour."

"How do you stand it down here all the time? Breathing dust?"

"I told you, I don't need to breathe anymore." I stood up and took a deep breath, I don't know why—just to feel the bellows of my body expand and contract around the stale, fumy air inside, even if there wasn't any point to it. Stretching felt good. I sat down at the edge of the desk, dislodging a pencil. She was pressed crumpled into the back of the couch. I said, "I'm sorry, this isn't much of a date."

"Do you eat?"

"Sometimes."

"I'll take you out to dinner," she said, "when you can leave this place. I'll take you somewhere really nice. And we'll sit outside, no matter how cold it is. And we'll feel curlicues of cool wind in our lungs. You'll love it."

I sat down at my Yamaha keyboard, twirling a few degrees from one side to the other on the slick black stool. My eyes closed. She said, "What should I do?"

"I'm fine."

"You look like you hated remembering that."

"I don't hate it. I just don't feel very much when I remember it. You know—my life was just starting to come together a little. I'd just started taking my shirt off in public." With my thumb I stroked middle C, the note invisible, silent, just a click of the weight in the keyboard, but it domed in my head, a perfect wave I could have bitten off from the other sounds in the room. I switched the keyboard on.

"And now you feel dysmorphic again."

"Dysphoric," I said, half laughing, a crazy little laugh. "Sorry, I'm not laughing at you. I used to read the word as *dysmorphic* too."

"But that's when you see your body as something it doesn't look like," she said, finally sounding a bit put out.

I lifted my hands to the keyboard. "Dysphoria is the opposite of euphoria. It's what happens when you see your body as *exactly* what it looks like. It comes from excess of awareness, not too little awareness. That's the term."

Then I played her the first movement of Beethoven's Piano Sonata no. 17, *Der Sturm*. I used to teach this piece often, and it comes to my hands automatically, springingly, one of the most elegant pieces of music I know in its design—like a person making a good argument and building, building, as more and more points come to them. Like parliamentary debate. This orderly and mannerly music is not what people associate with Beethoven, but that's what it always reminds me of when I'm inside it, like holding up my finger and saying, *And this! And you!* When I was done Elsie applauded, leaning forward, her cheeks pink, drumming her heels against the foot of the couch to fill in the blanks of the noise.

"Where did that come from?"

"A musical interlude," I said. "The best conversations need them."

CHAPTER 6

The Shalk Stalk

We had tacos across the street, at a place where the red grease runs down the yellow shells on top of the yellow tables against the red walls. People come in and yell, and there's a feeling of peculiar efficiency, a jostling pressure.

"So you died," said Elsie at last, as we finished eating.

My blood sugar wasn't any better, of course, but I did feel better having tasted something and scented fresh air, and I felt a little more aware of how overwhelmed I'd been.

I said, "Yes. So this pinback killed me. I was even current on my tetanus shot. I went to the doctor and they cleaned me up, I went home, et cetera. But sometimes people get it even if they're inoculated, and somehow I didn't make the connection when I woke up feeling all stiff and fucked-up. I've always had problems with my jaw—the joint of it. Too much clenching and grinding. One time my whole jaw got frozen into place a little misaligned—for two whole days, while I was in the middle of moving. So jaw problems were familiar, and I left it too long before I realized anything was really wrong. Then I almost immediately was in the hospital, and deteriorated pretty fast after that. Tetanus wears you out. In severe cases, they have to put nutritional fluids straight into you with a tube, because your muscles become constantly tense, and it's *work*. It's exercise. Your whole body tries to turn into an arch. I don't remember anything about all this. I remember the pin and I remember what happened after. I know I was on a ventilator. I know they called my mom. But mainly I remember waking up and knowing something was wrong, that I couldn't feel my body the way I used to. My body felt a little more abstract, and every part of it felt about the same as every other part."

"How's that?"

"I used to get input from all the parts of my body," I said. "You know how it is. Something itches. Something presses against your clothes. Something is too tight. Some muscle is tired. There's a corn. Now my whole body felt even and cool, sort of nerveless. And there was cardboard and tape slapped over the window, and I was in restraints. They'd put them on because they were afraid I'd be a danger to myself if I learned what had happened, or a danger to other people before they could explain the protocols. They imagined I had instincts that would overwhelm me." I felt the cold, cloudy flush again, in the center of my head. "It was the worst day of my life."

I felt her hand on mine; I jerked away and apologized, shaking the hand out as if I'd banged it on something. I put it deliberately back onto the table, and took hold of her wrist as if to guide it back on, but this time she pulled away.

"I'm sorry. This is hard for you to remember."

"Not your fault. I shouldn't be angry at you."

"Honey, it's never too soon in a relationship to get angry at me. What I think I've heard—is you could live a pretty long time. What I mean is that eventually—that worst day of your life could stay the worst, and it could be fifty or a hundred years later."

"I think the last is always the worst," I said. "Who said that one? But it's true, in a way. I mean, my body won't change that much, from this point. It won't age much. It will wear out more than anything, because it doesn't really rebuild itself the way yours does. Joints dry out into useless rubber. Skin goes papery. And eventually we all get careless. You know those people who are born unable to feel pain? They don't tend to live to see thirty. Vampires are kind of like that. There's not a really obvious upper limit on our lives. Theoretically, if you had all the money and resources in the world to help you stay out of the sun—if you were a vampire movie star, or a vampire king— with assistants to organize your life, and an architect to build you a lovely house without windows, and with doors that were airlocks, you could live hundreds of years. But the reason that people have always thought of us sort of as a legend is that the average life span of a person after they get vampirism is three and a half years."

"*Three . . . ?*"

"Because it's impractical to live the way we are," I said. "I'm really privileged, as we go. That's why they started infecting people who were dying of things like tetanus. It's like chemo; it'll buy you a few years. Sooner or later the sun will see us."

We went outside wiping our fingers on paper napkins, and she caught at my shoulder in the doorway and said, "Do you mind if I don't come back with you?"

"I might have thought enough for one night," I said. "That's fine. You didn't get enough sleep. And we only talked about me."

"Oh, I never want to talk about me. Never ever. I told you, I'm the least interesting person alive." Her cool lips on my jaw; she kissed me there. My hands rested on her polyester shoulders, feeling the little scratch of them like beard-scratch.

"I felt that way before I transitioned too."

"Stop it. Don't transition me." She pitched the joke perfectly, right at middle C, and I leaned in to kiss her more seriously, on the lips, tasting the spice in our mouths and intertwining my fingers with hers. I was still standing on the step of the restaurant, so we were the same height, or I was a little taller. She pulled away from me and fussed with the pocket of my T-shirt. "What are you going to do after we break up?"

"Are you negging me?"

"No! I mean—I misspoke. I mean after I leave for the night."

"I don't know. Play the keyboard more. I'm worried about what Florence is going to do tomorrow."

"You play so well. Did you ever teach?"

"I trained to be a concert pianist. Then I trained other people to be concert pianists. Then I needed health insurance."

"You play really, really beautifully," she said, her mouth generating another little fractal of phrases, something pretty that felt automatic, but I found myself wanting to zoom in on it and pull it apart anyway. We kissed once more and she walked off purposefully, as if she had somewhere to go, as if a camera were pulling up and up and watching her walk down the street.

At the archives, I found myself tidying. Not just my office, but the kitchen and break room, the reading room, the conference room where the collection was. I dusted, vacuumed, and cleaned away the crust of food that covered the break room table. I sprayed industrial cleaner that made everything smell like sunshine and pines. I imagined that smell being pumped into a VR headset that would give the rich vampire of the future a snatch of the hills. The only vampire who's ever been a king was Baudoin—Baldwin—of Jerusalem, and he lived two years before his blood boiled in him. A deliberate assassination. Someone threw open the shutter of his bedroom window, carved with crosses intertwined with pelicans, and by this murdered him in his sleep.

The first thing you noticed about *The Black Kite*, Tracy's novel, was that it filled a whole box, and that it was all starts and stops—swinging folders, carefully labeled, but in no order. The first draft of chapter two, the fifth draft of chapter six, "cuts," "misc." I picked one up at random, sliding a divider reflexively into the box to keep my place, and found to a quickening of my heart that it was set in the *Feet of Clay* universe. Autofanfiction!

Eurytheme excelled at creating empty men, and while Ivahim Zaduk was not empty, he was filled with the most casual stuff—scraps of omelet, coffee grounds, once-clear water used to clean a tub, and bits of bright broken glass. He was a clean ceramic jar with all this trash inside and you had to know him well to recognize that the theme was that it was a collection of colors: yellow, brown, blue, and colorless light. That was the only thing he was really interested in. Why?

He had never known why. He had been placed in a friendly, prosperous family that liked velvet and other soft cloth. He had a brother and a sister, but there was a gap between him and them. His parents treated him differently. They never touched him, and looked on his successes and failures alike without surprise. From an early age he knew he was coated with a special silence that repelled all comers. And so he became a dissociated man, which is to say a great appreciator of beauty. He never noticed a relevant detail. Instead, as a teacher castigated him

for not applying himself, he saw the greasy glass of the classroom win-
dow, looking out on the concourse. As a potential girlfriend made shy
overtures, he noticed the glare off her teeth. As people moved around
him on the concourse, he saw only their quivering molecular course, the
way it resembled the smashed dots of neutrinos coming to rest in a lab
after flying through planets and stars without incident. He never knew
how much Shalk worried about this, or how little Shalk understood
that Zaduk was as harmless as egg-white and as inert as glass. Beauty,
as Oscar Wilde said in one of his better moments, is that which has
nothing to do with you, and Zaduk knew beauty helplessly, adoringly,
because nothing in the world seemed to have much to do with him.

It went on like that. I can't say that it was bad; some of the
images were pretty striking.

But nothing happened in the whole book except *fretting*. Descriptions of characters I'd loved, whom I'd seen in action,
fighting and shooting and losing dreadful things that left holes
in their flesh—but this "book" was nothing but endless descriptions of their interiority, of a lifetime's worth of frozen
moments compressed into one little jar. The sense it gave was
of an overwhelming claustrophobia, an imprisonment in skin,
and above all a dirty shame.

Shalk let his hands flutter into his lap. He looked down into the city,
below him vertiginous and small, though not so small that this balcony
did not have a certain uncomfortable intimacy—he could make out the
carpeting down there.

This miha adventure was beating an old sore skin drum inside of him which said this: You have no detective mind. You are the hundredth of your name and this cannot be so. You sprang from the same seed that made all the Shalks, whose names are not changed between lives as the others are—the Shalk stalk, your ex-wife once said, and was there an irony in her mouth when she said this silly thing? You don't remember.

No. He was made from the flesh of the first. There was no fading, no degeneration, from that first perfect snapshot. And yet there was always an instant between him and others, when they realized he did not grasp the case as well as the detective Shalk ought to.

He was a good interrogator. He knew that. A sensitive musician of the human mind, a thoughtful assimilator of fact. He could follow the pink string of a theory, and he had a special power too: to look at everyone's cards, the card of Known Cowardice, the card of Old Crimes, all left scattered behind them in previous lives. He knew all about himself, that he was brilliant, although one Shalk had falsified evidence, and another had killed his partner, and so on and so forth: each old life had a crack in it, and after a while you assembled a pretty good collection of cracks and you could rearrange them to spell a word.

But there was no remarkable insight in him. He had spent so long looking for that insight that he did not even know what it was.

You would never know, from Tracy's descriptions of Shalk, why I'd devoted my whole youth to this character—why I'd spent my blushes on imagining his love affair with Zaduk. But then, you wouldn't know it from the show either. That version of Shalk was my own creation.

I no longer understand this love story I worked so hard to invent. Shalk's feeling for Zaduk is obviously chaste. The person he wants to fall in love with is himself. If Shalk solves the mystery of Zaduk, grasps the right glowing wire and learns why *this* Zaduk never became a killer, then he will know why he's a detective. He'll know what motivated the original Shalk to take up the work. Shalk doesn't get it at all; he's not in love with the city, takes no pleasure in controlling it by his intellect or the force of his hands. He was assigned cop at birth, that's all.

I'd dressed as Shalk once, when I was fifteen, at a *Star Trek* convention—back in the day, the *Feet of Clay* fans used to crash those cons a lot. I made his gray jacket from a suit jacket I'd thrifted, twisting it tight around my body to make it double-breasted. Underneath were black Express trousers with rick-rack hot-glued to the sides. I couldn't replicate Shalk's large pale head, with its dusting of gray hair like granulated sugar, but I pulled back my long hair and slid it into my collar.

In my bedroom mirror, the costume was thrilling. The jacket fell straight around my body, hiding my chest and my waist, and I'd found just the right black boots with points. I felt like a different person—not Shalk, of course, that would be childish, but strong and secret. The really important part was that no one knew it was me.

At the con, the ladies' room stalls were all full: women in crinolines, carefully lifting them up to pee. There was always a parade of Victorian reenactors at this con too. It was San Jose in the nineties, and every type of nerd came out to every type of event. So I went to the men's room, because after all I was *dressed as a male character*, and used a stall, feeling very illicit and pleased with myself.

When I came out of the stall, there was a second Shalk at the mirror next to me. He was perfect. Uniform tailored to his flat and massive body, a clean line down his forehead to his nose, and another from padded shoulders to jodhpured hips. His baldness and his height were clear and natural, the obvious course of a body.

He didn't glance back at me, even though we wore the same clothes. We must have looked very little alike in them, anyway—a man wearing five hundred dollars, a child wearing garbage. In my doubled-over jacket, I felt like a twist of cheap candy, a Tootsie Roll. He left before I did, and when I stepped back out into the hotel lobby, I saw him swallowed into the crowd and the cracked dazzle of natural light. I began to follow him.

I walked through solid television, people dressed as aliens all around me, drapery of latex and upholstery fabric. I followed the man's rolling shoulders to a panel on worldbuilding, one of the little writing panels that get attached to these big cons like burrs. He sat through the whole thing, legs crossed rather daintily, and then got up and left for the bar. I wasn't old enough to drink, so I left him there; there was nowhere to hide.

Surveillance, paranoia. That's what *Feet of Clay* was about. But Tracy somehow didn't know that; she just thought she was rolling out a load of characters, doing her job, and I honestly don't think that she saw the patterns in the stories. As I followed the man, I didn't know what I was doing either. I didn't look at him with pleasure, I didn't find him handsome, and as for a desire to be him, ah—even today, I don't feel that way about such men. The soul knows what's not possible.

I just wanted to *look* at him. I needed to commit him to my memory, from his chapped fingers, to the wax delicately applied to the insides of his ears, to the lobes of those same ears, which had been pierced for earrings. The sight of him frightened me as much as it pleased me—all my most opaque wishes, brought in a bloom to the surface—and when I finally left, it was because the bloom had choked me.

It came to me that this was what I really wanted of Shalk: to stare at a perfect reproduction. I wanted to see him in every detail, including the interior matter that didn't show up on TV, where every actor's face is a bubble around nothing. And now I'd seen that reproduction, and it was useless, because I was somehow unequipped to look at it right.

In an empty ballroom at the conference hotel there was a grand piano. I touched the keys. It was horribly out of tune, severed nerves and broken nose. Still, although I felt it would hurt this wounded thing further, I sat down and began to play. I stayed there, typing out Mozart's Piano Sonata no. 15 from memory, until I saw curious people starting to gather in the doorway, and then I got up and dashed through their bodies, feeling the solid thump of them as they tried to get out of the way, until I was outside.

That night, there was unusual activity in the archives. Usually there's no sound there, of course, but you can hear things—the *niki-tit-chat* of the climate control, whose pipes are faulty and tick agonizingly, and the clothy rub that underlies everything, the sound of paper straining against paper, which I don't think anybody but me can hear. It's a metaphor, that sound, but I also think it's very real. The heart makes a noise in the chest, and the tongue in the mouth, even though only we can hear them because our bodies are such perfect machines for the conduction of their own sound. So too I hear the sound of the archives. But tonight, everything was louder than usual. I heard the flap of papers in the reading room, where Tracy Britton's collection sat—the wind of climate control trying to lift and twist the corners of dog-eared pages, and the whine of the fluorescent lights that go on all night in there. A nervousness, a nerviness, a weary enervation in the air. Old products are creepy, and empty rooms are creepy, and that's because they don't conduct *sound* like new products—made of different things—or like rooms that are full. And over it all floated the smell of must and rust and vinegar, of moth damage and mothballs. Stronger than usual, and it made me feel weaker. I closed my eyes but could not sleep.

CHAPTER 7

Darya

Little nonprofits like ours don't really have HR; instead, we have Darya. She's a one-day-a-week contractor, a skinny young brunette with hair piled on top of her head and a plush face—she looks as if she has carefully placed pieces of cotton in her cheeks to stretch out their smile lines. I'd always liked her, as I always like young women who have to struggle to be taken seriously. I never exactly was one, but I feel a core sympathy for them.

"Sol," she said. "How are you doing?"

"I'm well," I said. "I imagine Florence has spoken to you."

"She has," said Darya, and slipped one paper under another on her desk. Darya's office was locked with a special lock that my keys couldn't get into. I didn't snoop in people's offices, but I still found it a little intimidating that if I wanted to snoop in hers, I couldn't. "And I think Florence has a history of strong reactions to things, but that doesn't mean I don't have to ask you some questions."

"Okay."

"Have you been staying in your office overnight sometimes?" Her voice was, for the first time, hesitant.

"Sometimes I work late and stay overnight."

"That would be fine," she said, with a note of apology in her voice, "except that there's a security camera over the door, and I've reviewed some of the film."

"Oh, God."

"You can't stay here, Sol. I'm sympathetic to your problems, but the office isn't zoned for people to live."

"I'm not alive," I said, feeling an anger inside me coalesce into something rubbery and hard. "I'm just sort of a body that's kept going through artificial resuscitation, and might do for another few years yet. Look, I can't go out if there's any sun."

"You've told me that many times, Sol, and I listened."

"In the summer, if I live somewhere else, even in the city, which I can't afford because I'm an archivist, that means I have to come to work at three in the morning and I can't leave until ten anyway. I'd be risking death for no actual reason except propriety."

"Okay," said Darya, who had pulled away from me and was sitting with her shoulders flat against her chair. "Bear in mind that this was not my decision and is not my fault, and I *know* all this. You need to find a place to live that isn't this office. *You* need to solve the practical problems involved. I can't do that for you. And I know it's going to be difficult, but you are going to make people so uncomfortable. You've already made Florence incredibly uncomfortable."

"That's her base state, Darya, don't pretend you don't know that. Especially around trans people, who are a protected class."

"You're *not* going to tell the HR lady that someone's discomfort is baseless," said Darya.

"Still a protected class."

"Do you want to talk about that? Because there's discomfort and there's crossing a line in how you react to it, and I haven't seen her cross a line—unless you have. I don't see everything."

"Not a line as such," I said. "She mostly just talks about how she wouldn't want to transition, which isn't *necessarily*, like, pointed."

"Exactly. And whatever I might think about that personally, I am going to take very seriously the fact that you left a . . . prosthetic on your desk in the office. At least close your door if it's a time when you can imagine coworkers being in."

"That room is the only home I have."

"That's exactly why you need to leave," she said. "Sorry, not *quit*, not leave, we like you here and you do good work, but the fact that you've come to think of it as your home, Sol—and five minutes ago it was just, 'I work late and stay here sometimes.' I've told you everything I need to tell you. Why don't you take a walk and cool off?"

"Because I can't go outside or I'll die."

"Take a walk in the hall."

I got up, but didn't go anywhere. I said, "You know, the ADA requires that you make a reasonable accommodation for people who are sick. I'm sick, and I didn't choose to be."

"A reasonable accommodation, Sol."

"It's reasonable to ask me to go home for the eight hours that it's completely dark in summer? Or, I mean, to commute home for an hour, so I'm home for six hours—"

"And besides," she broke in, "we don't have to do that; we're too small a company. We don't have to accommodate anything. We do what we've done so far because it's the decent thing to do, but we can't afford to open ourselves up to all kinds of liability—"

"What have you done so far?"

"You'd better take a walk, Sol."

She was right; I needed to take a walk in the hall. Not that I was any happier, or less angry, after I did it—but I was more able to be quiet.

I wasn't able to see back then how *stupid* it was to leave the packer out, and how it would look to anyone who came in that day. Of course, I'd never meant Florence to see it; even if I'd wanted to make her uncomfortable, I knew all I had to do was exist. No, I'd just forgotten I wasn't at home. On Saturdays, when nobody comes in, my office seemed to change locations with the click of a light. I usually close the door too, and had only left it open because Elsie had called early, when everything was in disarray.

I can say all that, but all it proves is that I had broken down years ago, and instead of calling for help, I'd chosen to disassemble the car and build a shack out of it at the side of the road. If you need to make excuses that come down to, *You wouldn't have been upset about my shack if you hadn't driven by*, your life isn't working.

I sat down at the conference table to start processing again. I had a dozen things I had to do before this back-burner task—"a dozen things," you imagine soft crumbled rubber, things with extra ridges and lips of rubber left behind by a badly calibrated machine, improperly dyed and barely recognizable. You know, "things." I was still angry and struggling to concentrate, and processing was an excuse to put my headphones on and listen to punk music while cautiously picking at folders. So far, no more of them held inexplicable sap, and I hadn't been able to bring myself to ask Elsie about that.

The screenplays had been mostly episodes of the show, with some failed pilots, or scripts on spec, which I'd set aside to read at night later. That's one of the pleasures of being a night archivist; you get to *read the things*, in a way that people in the archives during the day never do.

Oh, I won't say that I spent most of my nights productively.

I often read light books, or watched a Mobius strip of television, and when I wanted to read a heavier book, I rode BART around and looked at different parts of the city. I pretended I was commuting, and that's how you get the conveyor belt of thought going, the feeling that you are coursing around, feeling ball bearings rolling beneath the rubber under your feet. Sometimes I went to bars and sat in the corner. I don't like drinking, but I like bars, especially their light, which in some bars is wet and in some is hot and toothsome. I like the way the lights in bars tend to be amber, and the pinball tables are black and red, and the pool tables are green, and everything in there is some kind of specialized table that's for anything but eating and drinking, because I've had to learn to form myself around activities that aren't eating and drinking. It gets so boring sometimes—not having to organize your life around anything. And I go to a lot of movies.

But sometimes, at night, I stay in, and I read the things. I let people's self-justifying letters, and their anguished diary entries, and their drawings for tattoo plans, and their board meeting minutes (dry and salty like a cracker), and their ephemera (crackling and fine like popcorn), their collections of T-shirts and buttons, their sugar-rough china dolls and plasticizer-leaking dildos, their audiotapes of meetings and interviews with friends. Very little in archives is smooth like butter; archives are all crunch. And, as I've said, all poison. The plastics alone can kill you. We think of plastics as eternal, because people my age were raised to be concerned about landfills, but the truth is that we outlive most of our plastics, especially the PVC. They don't degrade into anything good, but they do degrade, and when they go, they go to slime.

It is a pleasure to read the things. The queer kids a few years ago liked to talk about trash, like Oscar the Grouch might talk about trash—I'm trash, I'm a heap, a pile, in a Dumpster, cartoon banana peels, a soft carpet of dead salad. This just means that I'm very interested in something, invested in a fandom, or I'm too depressed to clean but I'm taking pleasure in the Quentin Crisp fact that never cleaning doesn't make me any dirtier, after a while. But archives really are trash. Everything in an archives is something that somebody thought about throwing away and didn't. To play in the garbage chute, to find out about all these old traumas and dramas—that's where the glee comes in, a glee like having someone scoop up the papers behind you and let them flutter down on your head.

CHAPTER 8

Series 2:
Show Bibles

DEAD COLLECTIONS is a different kind of series. It's about a lonely, horny archivist who begins — tentatively at first, but with increasing confidence — to make inroads into understanding a collection whose main subject is dead. The tone of the show is a peculiar combination of boredom and fascination. The camera is always sitting with Sol Katz in the reading room, as he refolders and relabels an endless collection of what archivists simply call "materials." Occasionally he gets up for coffee, but the camera stays on the table the whole time. This is not Sol's favorite part of his job, but it is the most satisfying part, the part that makes him feel like if he dies now or later, he'll have left something behind other than ashes and clothes. Vampire ash isn't fluffy dust, as people

imagine it to be; nor does it resemble the
"cremains" that are sent to us from the
crematorium, which are really just pulverized
bones. It is heavy and flaky, like cigarette ash,
or like fungi. Some have compared the physical
texture to crumbled gorgonzola cheese. You're
uncomfortably aware that there's fat in it. Sol
is not eager to become cheese, which is part of
the reason he spends all of his time in this
basement, working assiduously and trying not to
have anyone notice that he's living here! He has
dismally failed. Fuck! Let's meet the cast.

SOL KATZ

Sol is a trans man, but it's fine for him to
be played by a cis woman. He doesn't pass
anyway. (Sorry! I know the language of
passing is extraordinarily problematic! This
is the headspace Sol's in right now, as he
sits here with his headphones on, slowly
crying thick cold tears.) Sol is the dumbest
asshole in existence, and rude to women
besides. If he'd tried harder to make the
piano happen — even fully committed to
teaching, much less to his abortive concert
career — he would literally be alive today,
without tetanus, without vampirism, with a
glowing transsexuality whose biggest concern
vis-à-vis the sun would be its potential
conflicts with his acne medications. At five-
two with a limited wingspan, perhaps he was
never going to be a world-class pianist
anyway, but he did love it once, before the

burnout got too terminal; he could practice
for a full workday in a way that he cannot
work now without the headphones and the
tears. Get up, Sol, and blow your nose!
You're dripping on the files.

TRACY BRITTON

Tracy "Trace" Britton died at fifty-eight in
her sleep from an aneurism. Her wife, Elsie
Maine, rolled over in their soft dryer-pad-
smelling flannel sheets to embrace her in
the morning and found her cold, which SOL,
YOU SHOULD PROBABLY NOT THINK ABOUT, WITH
REGARD TO WHETHER KISSING YOU IS SOME KIND
OF PTSD-BASED SELF-HARM. Tracy mostly
appears in this narrative as she was between
1992 and 1996, which is to say a tough dyke
in her thirties, with sandy hair that forms
a heavy lock over one eye, and dark nineties
makeup sometimes, an enviable five-foot-
seven. She should be played by a cis woman
who looks like someone has carefully cast
her as a dyke with an eye to making the show
not TOO unappealing to heterosexual guys.
Katee Sackhoff wouldn't be bad, but only in
the pilot of *Battlestar Galactica*, with the
short dirty-blond hair — God! *That* was dyke
energy, but in a body that all the boys were
fighting over, and so in retrospect, that's
gay trans man energy too. Let's take a
moment, just a moment, to take out our
greedy little phone and Google Image that.

God!

The thing is, Sol is beginning to suspect that Tracy is a terrible person. Or rather, that she might not be a big enough character to be terrible, but that she's not *good*. Granted, Sol has only been through the scripts and show bibles so far, but he's surveyed the correspondence, and so he has a sneak-ahead peek at the person who seems to have been the love of Tracy's life, and it's not Elsie. It's Ali Payne, for whom she was forever writing parts, most prominently the part of Kate in *Clay*. (*Clay* is so-called, of course, because of the aliens. Don't imagine that it's called that because Tracy was secretly a terrible person! It doesn't seem to be much of a secret.)

A serial cheater, is the main thing. Tracy slept with Ali Payne for most of her life. She'd go on business trips to L.A. during her marriage to Elsie for no purpose other than to fuck Ali Payne, and to feel bad about it. While she was with Ali, she seduced Elsie; while she was with Ali, she also slept with guest stars, junior writers, anyone who needed something from her. That much is obvious from the letters, which often reused the same protestations of love. They were typed. Tracy typed on a manual typewriter, and she kept carbons.

Why did everyone want to fuck her? That's what's confusing to Sol. She was hot and had one good idea, and affable, I guess. Loved the romance of being caught between two women, and got strong off of it. Why was she so good at surrounding herself with

interesting, vital women and turning them
into husks? Like some sort
of . . . . *vampire*?

ALI PAYNE

The other major character in this story, so
far — Elsie is barely in it. After they moved
in together, Elsie and Tracy went into one
of those paradoxical archival lacunae, where
you're so close that you stop generating
letters, papers, anything but "financial and
administrative documents." Sometimes the last
words a couple writes to each other are
their signatures on the marriage license.
Letters come from longing, which means that
archives run on longing. You make less to
archive once you get what you want. But Ali
is around from the beginning. What's strange
about this — oh, I should do something,
nominally, to nod to this "show bible"
format — all right — Ali is medium height,
should be played by a cis woman, good
cheekbones and strong jaw. Polished skull on
a whole. With long hair she looks leonine;
with short hair she just looks a little
truncated, unfinished. In *Clay* she plays Kate
Vettner, unlocker of a hundred thousand
closets, genteel leaver of the key on the
bed. Kate is not a great part, less fun than
some of the parts Tracy has written for her
in all these many bibles. (The first female
basketball player to play in a men's league!
A women's college professor with a tragic

secret! Someone who can shift gender — now, that's interesting; clearly Tracy had seen *Ranma* 1/2 by that point, but was trusting that nobody with greenlighting power had.) But Ali is a great actress. She has barely been heard from since '98, maybe because of being associated with so iconic a part as Kate, maybe because of homophobia, maybe because Ellen DeGeneres came out first and there was only room for one at the time, but maybe — maybe —

CHAPTER 9

Can You Ever
Forgive Me?

At the end of the week, when Elsie showed up for our second date—an hour late, because of an Archive of Our Own board meeting, and in a heavy businesslike sweater she was still struggling to take off when the elevator opened—she kissed me and said, "You look exhausted. That's not an insult. It's Byronic."

"Mmm."

Her hand was pressed to my side, and the contact through my red-and-black-striped sweater felt infinitely reassuring.

"Did you look for a new place to live?"

I tried to say, *No,* or *I couldn't,* but I couldn't speak. I shook my head. She ran the tip of her thumb beneath my eye and said gently, "I love this shiny spot, right here. The lines under your eyes are almost like gold."

I pressed my face to her broad shoulder. God, I love a girl you can rest on. I loved the way she'd placed her hand too—the side just above the hip is one of my favorite parts of my body, because it's one of the ones that's changed the most. No more sharp dip in, all straight and soft muscle now.

"It's not quite sunset yet," she said. "The sun's gone, but there's light in the sky. You can't go out in that, can you?"

"Not yet, no."

The offices were empty, but she broke contact with me and nudged the door shut anyway, and locked it. It was impossible not to see the intent in the motion. I said, "Wait."

She stopped, and looked at me politely.

"Are you going to kiss me again?"

"Yeah," she said. "We're gonna fuck in here, actually."

Whether she hoisted me up, or I pushed myself up, I ended up sitting on my desk so that we were the same height, kissing her fiercely. It seemed all right to be reckless now. Nothing, I imagined, could get any worse.

She was crying, suddenly, and I pulled apart from her, remembering the obituary I'd read and all that my imagination had added to it since. I kept my cold hand cupping her chin and then dropped it. She said, "I'm sorry."

"You don't need to be. I think we're both messes right now."

"God, I was being so cool—you must think I'm insane."

"Elsie, grief is weird. I get it."

"How did you know I was thinking of her?"

"Because I'm cold," I said.

"Oh. Oh, no." She wiped more tears with the heel of her hand. "I just miss her. I like you, and you didn't ask for this, and I miss her."

On impulse I kissed her wet cheek, and in the midst of the kiss I flicked my tongue out and tasted the salt. No foundation on her face today, no lipstick on the generous mouth.

"Sol."

"Mhm?"

"Can I touch you under your shirt?"

The request was so sweetly vague, so unexpectedly shy, that my "Okay" came out small and hot. She slid her hands up my hips and they met behind my back. I closed my eyes, and in my mind I was formulating another small protest—this was the exact activity that I had gotten into trouble for doing, it was what Florence thought I had done, but as I watched, the phrases just disappeared, like a clicked dialogue box.

"You're thicker than you look."

"Thanks."

"God, you feel good. You're a beautiful guy."

I kissed her a little more strongly and shifted, just to let her know that she was between my thighs against the desk. I was rewarded with a stronger smell of her perfume; she was sweating a little. I pressed closer to the heat of her breasts. I let my hand cup one of them lightly, through her dress, and when she moved toward me I took that as permission to slide my hand inside her bra and feel its weight. Her skin was, God, so soft, almost insubstantial in its softness, skin like cold cream on a makeup counter. I kissed her, and pressed my tongue to the tip of her front tooth.

We kissed some more on the sofa, over which I'd spread a blanket; she was coming apart under me, her thigh parting the flap of her wrap dress, and it was all I could do not to thrust myself in agony against it, against anything that came to hand, and come right away. Her hands were sliding up and down my back in a way that felt less and less controlled. I was just running my own hand up her inner thigh when she said, "Drink from me."

"I, uh, I can't do that," I said.

But the truth had thudded into me, loud and heavy, bursting through the edge of my skull: I *could* do that. I had never wanted to do it before. I didn't want to now, but something inside me that was as automatic as the ridged lining of my throat, as automatic as the course of my blood, was *ready* to do it, and was being rushed forward like a body in a crushing crowd. I could feel a diamond of pain under my gums, the two needle-teeth that press out through the roof of my mouth when I'm tired or horny or halfway through my transfusion, or sometimes for no reason at all.

"Please. I want you to. I really want to know what it's like."

"I shouldn't."

"Do you want me to make you?" she said lightly, and I pressed myself to her thigh after all and said, "You have to make me want to." She rolled over and pressed me against the back of the sofa, and our eyes met as she brought her hand slowly to my mouth and nose, to cover it and cut off my breath. I closed my eyes and leaned into it, kissing the palm fiercely, gagging a little on a gulp of air I'd forgotten I didn't have to take. Our eyes met again, and then, dazed with desire and no longer certain who was asking what of whom, I felt her pull her hand away. We pressed our foreheads together and she closed her eyes. Then her white neck was in my mouth, pressed to it, and I had broken the skin and I was drinking fast and hard.

I felt wild and accelerated, and as I drank I felt myself bucking up against her, needing to drink and needing to come with equal urgency—I couldn't stop one without the other, I couldn't do one without the other. The blood rushed into me like a hot liqueur, and I was drunk on it, didn't even taste it, just felt it heating me up, wings beating in my belly, in my veins. I took two gulping breaths of blood—I took all of her inside me—and then I came, God, I came harder than I've ever come, my body pressed against hers with all of its power, and the hot maddened blood filling my guts and pressing up through my arteries, plunging into my heart like a needle, pushing against my brain. Felt every nerve in my body at once. All this came with extraordinary clarity; I had life inside of me, and it had made me very drunk. When I looked at her again she did look as if she were wearing makeup; a delicate flush had come to her cheeks, her mouth was reddened, and a soft narcotic haze was in her eyes and around her damp lashes.

"You're hot," she said. "You're feverish. You're as hot as if you were alive."

I touched my chest, and it was true, I was hot as blacktop, hot as a wire, and I rolled back and away from her to feel it more fully, and she moaned in annoyance and said, "For fuck's sake finish me off, you're killing me."

"What do you want me to do?"

"Fucking give me your—no. Your mouth."

So I teased and sucked until she came, and then lay, head on her pubic bone, feeling her breathe. I was still hot, more so than I'd been in fact, sweating—and it was the clear smooth sweat of the living, which I missed so much. We were both soaked with it, and I closed my eyes in relief, because I knew it meant I hadn't made her sick. Afterward we lay quietly for a long time, her sleeping off the languor and me full of energy but trying to keep it inside. I felt wild, absurd, wolfish more than vampiric, the blood in me softening and thickening into something that ran slow in my sluggish veins. After an hour I was only warm, as a person should be warm, and I finally roused myself and sat up at the edge of the couch. She was sleeping deeply, her dress unwrapped and still around her flower-framed shoulders.

In the air, I sensed something a little sour. Under the smell of the perfume, a bile, something biological. At first I thought it was one or the other of us, an unwashed body, but this was purer, more vinegary, with the distressing probiotic aliveness of sewage. I got up and put on my bathrobe and treaded cautiously into the archives office proper, noticing with a shudder its professional familiarity and the delusion it had taken to pretend I wasn't at work—at heart I am not a subversive man, that's why I wasn't a top-rank pianist. The smell was unsettling. It put me off balance. The air was thick. Behind me there was the rustle of leather and then she came out, closing her dress.

"Are you feeling all right?" I asked her anxiously.

"Oh, I feel good. Just like I gave blood, maybe."

"I didn't know I could do that," I said blankly, only now I recognized how dissociated I was, how vague. "I had no idea. God, what did we *do*? I know I shouldn't have—I could have given you what I have."

"I made you do it," she said absentmindedly. "What is this *vibe* this place has at night? It's creepy."

I was so swamped with shame that I couldn't have told her anything about it. Even the smell seemed lessened. I said, "I need to wash up."

"I like you that way," she said, and touched my stiffened hair. "Let's go out on our date. I'm sorry about the spoilers—I mean, I spoiled the ending."

"I could have made you sick."

"But you didn't. Not tonight."

I covered my face, rubbed my eyelids with my finger and thumb. The shame was pressing against the blood inside me. I almost sobbed, at the feeling, at the hot, thin blood.

"Hey," she said softly. Her hand was on my back. "May I kiss you one more time?"

I lifted my face up, and we kissed, and the kick of shame—good shame, the shame of getting what you need—lasted until we got upstairs.

I reveled in the way the warmth got trapped in the fleece that lined my sweatshirt and reflected gently back into my skin, like light. The blood seemed to glow in my belly, where plenty of it had not yet left; it was an oil powering me, like the wick of a candle lit up in my flesh. I had to move carefully to keep that candle from being swamped with wax and going out. I felt weary, languorously weary as she had been languorous. In moments, our bodies or hands bumped against each other as we walked close together over the glittering sidewalk.

Somehow we got to the Metreon, where we'd been planning to see *Can You Ever Forgive Me?*—all this happened in 2018. At the Metreon you see your movie from an immobile position, in an absurd and rather kinky red recliner. We were alone in the back row, and so after watching the first half hour with our forearms pressed in each other's hands, we raised the armrests between us and I cuddled into her side. I was surprised to find I didn't mind being smaller than Elsie—nothing about it made me feel less. It was only as if I were very close to her, as if her body were magnified.

It was a good film and we both watched it with surprising attention, catching the snap of the dialogue and Melissa McCarthy and Richard E. Grant's quick and sad delivery, the way she only fails to get away with stealing in the archives because she can't make small talk with the archivist (accurate!), but mainly my impression was of all the light in the film, that glassy glossy New York light that hurtles down through the trees onto Melissa, or reflects at her off the dazzle of the river, the light that she absolutely cannot see.

At dinner, I asked for a cup of hot tea while Elsie ordered pasta and wine.

"Are you sure you don't want anything? I hate being the only one eating."

"I'll have . . ." I said, but food still sounded unbearable—like shit, compared to the glowing efflorescence inside me. I couldn't contaminate it, but ordered a bowl of potato soup to stir and fuss at anyway, and sipped my tea.

"So you've never bitten anyone before?" she asked me softly.

"No," I said. "They've always told me not to."

"You've softened your stance a lot from 'I shouldn't.'"

"It feels too good," I allowed. "And you asked. Did you know you'd ask?"

"I didn't *plan* to. But I hang out a little on vampire Twitter, and nobody there will ever admit it, but I know they do it. I was curious. I'd heard it's a high."

"And is it?"

"You couldn't tell?"

"I was too high myself."

Her fingertips lingered on her throat. "It's narcotic. To have your mouth in my neck, desperate, greedy, and I think there's a real drug involved too. Like mosquitoes have, to stop you from feeling them until they're gone. Only this one just made me feel loved-up and sleepy. I should tell you that I *did* want to fuck you all up and down before I knew you were a vampire."

"I know you did," I said. "I wanted to fuck you all up and down the moment we met, but I was shaking your hand, and I thought, well, one thing at a time."

She looked down and gave a private smile. "To tell you the truth, I always liked guys," she said. Then the food came, and as she ate, her color started coming back—she had been pale under the flush, and looked a little wan. "I just felt wrong when I was with them, if that makes sense."

"Oh, it makes perfect sense. That's how I always felt."

"Are you trying to recruit me to your transsexualized identity again?"

"Oh, definitely."

"It took me a long time to get that you can call yourself whatever you like—and *lesbian* felt best in 1995 and it felt best in 2005 and now *bi* feels better. But that doesn't cover how complicated it is, or all the reasons to avoid something. Some people don't fuck guys because guys don't move them. Some people don't feel safe with guys. I didn't fuck them because I didn't want their hands on me, even though I wanted my hands on them."

"It's true," I said, "I never really used my hands."

"You're different. And it's not because you're trans. And I don't think it's just because 'I like butches.' People spend so much time and energy trying to explain the pattern of their attraction, like they're playing a *round* of *Set*, and maybe all I can say is that you're different from most other guys in that I want you."

I leaned back to stretch, and almost gasped at how fresh it felt, the long muscles in my arms filling with blood, that unique almost orgasmic tingle in my back. "That's very gratifying to hear."

"God, you really are like this, aren't you?"

"Yes."

She pushed her plate an inch aside. "Can I talk to you about Tracy a little more?"

"Yes. God, all those nineties dykes had to have names like cheerleaders."

"Oh, I know. I know a Suzie dyke and a Jessica dyke and a Brandi dyke. With a *z*, with an *i*. And I think I also know a dyke who transitioned and goes by Rhys now, but his old name was the silliest of all."

"We do tend to swing the pendulum all the way around," I said. "I was talking to someone on Twitter once about how it's always the Carrie-to-Caleb transition, it's always Samantha-to-Saul, and he said *Assigned Sex in the City*."

"I love that."

"Wish it were mine. Anyway, now we're all named after prophets."

"Even you?"

"*Absolutely*. Solomon is one of the forty-eight prophets, per the Talmud. There's room to name a lot of trans men in there."

"I suppose I can't ask you your old name?"

"I don't say it aloud," I said. "It's pretty soon before Solomon. In the Bible, I mean, in terms of number of pages."

"David?"

"No. What were you going to say about Tracy?"

Elsie's face clouded over for a moment. "I was going to say, it was so different from being with you. Being with you was easy. Tracy couldn't fuck me without teaching me something. She taught me the shape of my body and she made me like it—I know that sounds fucked-up—but I didn't know how to like it, until she made me. I mean. It was consensual. I said yes. But I had to be held under for a while until I realized I could breathe water."

"That sounds like a very powerful experience," I said, trying not to sound too polite.

"It was. But I still wasn't breathing air. Did anyone else ever make you feel like that? Before you transitioned?"

"A little," I said, "but nobody ever taught me to like it. I have had my share of educational sex, though."

"Yeah?"

"I paid someone," I said. "Just to help me understand a few more things."

"Really?"

"I gave piano lessons. It seemed natural to get sex lessons."

"Sex lessons," she repeated. "That's very librarianlike of you."

"No, no, as a librarian, I just Google things. This was more like *consulting* a librarian."

"Did it help?"

"You're more qualified to answer that than me."

"Well, then—it did."

"Thank you."

She was staying the night in a hotel, and I went upstairs with her and we fucked again. I was still warm and tingling and when it was done we had a bath together. I had never felt so starry-eyed over someone; maybe it was the blood doing some other opaque work, but this particular evening, things had just come together like the two walls of water in the Red Sea that drowned Pharaoh and his thousand objections and concerns. It was thrilling just to look at her hand on my knee, the pale dimples against my brown leg-fur. I didn't leave until an hour before first light, which for me is as dangerous and out-of-character as passing someone hard and fast on a mountain road. At the door she kissed me, and smoothed my wet hair.

"I wish you could visit me sometime."

"How far's Marin?"

"An hour, but my house is—I could never make it safe for you."

"Still, it's winter. I could come up at night pretty safely. But I know you don't drive then."

"Thank you for saying *don't*, not *won't* or *can't*. Because it really is—I can't even think of it. Well—we figured this much out."

"What's it like there?"

"Oh," she said, and gave me a melancholy look that made my heart slow for a moment, pump her blood in a quick gulp and then a slow one. The ecstasy came to me once again that I had her blood inside of me. The Red Sea, indeed, and I was glad to drown. "God, I wish you could see it in the day. It's all light. It's one of those glass-wall houses that architects love to build and nobody could bear to live in except that they're off in the woods."

"Could bear! I could have borne it once."

"I'll take you there. I'll find a way." She kissed me once more, kissed my forehead and my nose. "Does your name make you angry now? 'Sol'?"

"All the time. I thought seriously of changing it."

"It suits you, though. You're sweet and bright." I was still pinned tight against the door, and I felt her hand on the knob and then I was half falling into the cold of the hall, away from the heat of her body. I held on to her for a moment. "Get home," she said. "Don't die."

CHAPTER 10

Vampire Support Group

When I woke up, I felt good. I yawned and said Elsie's name aloud, and then stopped, feeling the word hover over my mouth like a feather, because there was a burr in my throat I wasn't used to; I felt that gift that early testosterone had made me used to for a time, of a few lower notes than I had ever been given before. It was the first real movement in transition that I'd felt in years. I sat up and tried my voice again, and this time I knew it was real.

Things seemed possible this morning. I googled "vampire support group" and found one that met downtown at ten o'clock Sunday nights. I was sure that there were people who had to figure out how to live and work, and all I really had to do was ask what others did. I saw now that I had been hiding for too many years. In the meantime, still drunk on joy, I sat down and touched the glassy keys of the keyboard, delighting in the way that my hot fingers left soft prints on the plastic—grease and steam, all the things a warm human body or a warm machine make.

The reason I rarely played these days wasn't dramatic. I just couldn't take pleasure in it anymore. And there was no point in doing it if I couldn't do it exceptionally well, and by now I played at the level of a pretty good amateur and no more. I also missed the piano, the instrument itself. The keyboard I kept in my office, under a rustling plastic dustcover, couldn't ever be more than a simulation of a piano. It was a good one, with weighted keys, but when you play well you play the *whole* piano; you play the resonances inside the lid and the ways the strings buzz and purr under the hammers, you play the echo of the pedals and the length of time you can make them ring.

It doesn't take skill to make the sounds of the keys. I think it's Stephen Fry who says playing the piano is just pushing buttons in order. But it takes skill to play the resonance and the weight and the pushback of the piano, and to accept the responsibility of filling a room with sound with one hammer stroke. My voice is a scratchy, nasal tenor, but my piano is a bass-baritone, and to me, he is everything.

Still, for the next couple of hours I did something very uncharacteristic. I played and I lost myself in the music, where I'd been accustomed for many years to find myself. Or rather, to get so lost that I found something. I found nothing that day, but it was all right.

The support group met in the community hall of a church in the lower Haight, brown wood of that chocolaty flat hue popular in the seventies. Younger cis women and older cis men, mostly, who looked like they worked in the trades—I wondered if they were the recipients of the tetanus cure. There must have been twenty of them there. I took my seat and rocked my feet back and forth on their heels, impatient and strangely stuffy-headed.

The moderator, Jim, was a handsome older guy with one of those titanic, hypertrophied varsity jaws. He gave the usual introduction—I've done support groups too, for trans people mostly—and we went around the circle with our names and how long we'd been sick, and our concerns. When the circle got to me, I said a little uncertainly, "My name is Sol, I've been sick five years, and I'm having a good day—I guess I just came for practical advice. I work in an archives, so I'm always in the basement and don't have to worry about the sun, and I've actually been squatting at work for a while because it seems pointless to live anywhere else. But they found out, and I want to know what other people even do."

The tenor of the room shifted then, and I didn't realize why until later—I thought it was my visible transness (visible at best), my voice, something about archives, something about squatting. I know now that it was because I said I'd been sick for five years. When the introductions finished, Jim said, "Sol, can I talk to you outside of the group for a minute?"

"Sure—I mean, I'm sorry—was I supposed to pay? Or register?"

"Come outside. Dashiell, please take over till I'm back."

We sat down on the church's back steps, which led down into an alley. It must have been cold, but I didn't feel it anymore. The fresh blood had worn off that much. Jim didn't put on the sweater he had tied around his shoulders; he sat there in his polo, basking in the streetlight as if it would give his skin a tan, a sunlit glow.

"Five years, huh?"

"Yes, a little over."

"And how have you adjusted to it?"

"I haven't," I said, and the saying shook something loose in me. "I've been a mess. I've been miserable. Until the other day."

"Uh-huh." He shifted in place on the step. "Are you actually a vampire, Sol?"

There was a breath in the air. I said, "Why wouldn't I be? Am I in the wrong support group—is it for people with—another kind?"

"Look," said Jim, having apparently come to a decision. "If you are a vampire—and I don't know how you've gone five years without knowing this—you've been drinking from a person. We can tell, Sol, we can practically smell it on you. You're *warm*. You're pink like a rare steak. And we can't have anyone in group who drinks from people, okay?"

"I don't drink from people," I said, but the flush—the real flush—betrayed me. "I just drank from a person. For the first time. Consensually—she asked me to do it. And I won't do it again."

"You will do it again. Once people start doing it, they do it again. You idiot, man, this is a *recovery* group. You don't come drunk to AA, why do you think you can come blood-drunk to a vampire thing?" He was getting up already, but I felt too rubbery on my feet, suddenly, to get up too. I touched, I don't know why, the jeans over his ankle. He jerked his leg away from me. "I don't want to talk to you."

"I am not going to do it again," I said fiercely. "I was turned on and tired—"

"You'll be turned on and tired again."

"I can't put her at risk like that again, but she asked—"

"If someone asks you to help them kill themselves, do you do it?"

"In Oregon, yeah!"

"Look," he said, and then, I don't know how it happened, but he wound up and kicked me hard in the stomach—a martial artist's kick, square with the foot. I forgot I didn't have to breathe; I almost retched. He kicked me again, in the side, as I crouched on my hands and knees.

"Why?"

"I'm not doing this for fun," he hissed at me. "But you are going to bring all kinds of shame on all of us by behaving this way, and you may as well kill yourself instead of helping your girlfriend die, no matter if you live in—what was that, in *Oregon*?"

I couldn't move, I couldn't speak. I felt crumpled and old.

"If you'd done this to me," he said, "I wouldn't feel it. I wouldn't throw up, I wouldn't have a headache, I wouldn't bruise. You should remember that, if you're tempted to do that again, and you will be. Remember that I'll be here to make sure you get the shit kicked out of you, and that if you do it, you'll feel it."

He walked away, the crunch of gravel on the steps loud and hard. I lay there for a little while, feeling at my face, which right now seemed a soft puffy mask over my skull. Then I rolled over, feeling solidly wretched, a rock tumbler of pain.

Jim was right, of course, I thought, as I lay there in the dark. Time seemed to pass very quickly; a hovering star was there, and then it was swept away behind the black mass of the building next door. I could feel the strength and energy I'd gotten from the blood draining away into a million little holes of paresthesia. He was right. I was a dead person, kept alive by an artificial process that kept me in a state like hypothermia, kept me frozen in more ways than one—stiff, preserved, chilly. Without my transfusions I'd die and without my darkness I'd die. My body was shaking. I felt full of sand and water. I hadn't been breathing at all, but suddenly my breath came audible and rhythmic, like panic, like orgasm, and then it stopped. I stopped breathing. I went still.

The group ended, and I heard everyone leaving the front of the church, dispersing into smaller conversations like flying sparks, then vanishing. I had, in a peculiar way, never felt more alive than this. Everything was immediate, and I noticed it all: the echoes of all the little sounds of the city, the hum of halogen, the hot spritz of urine. The tunings and detunings of cars. It came to me then that I really ought to be dead.

From delight to despair: a remarkable day, one long trip down. Blood-drunk and hungover: yes, it was like that, but there's really nothing like the drunkenness of hope after you've been in despair a long time, and there is no hangover—no hypercorrection, no black wall of a sinking ship after the lights are drowned and before the people go—like despair after hope. Somehow I got up and went down to BART, and sat there drinking water from a bottle whose plastic was as thin as skin, which I'd picked up in a vending machine. I rode all night from Embarcadero to the airport and back, and when dawn threatened, I shifted to the muzzy holding pattern of Embarcadero to 24th Street Mission, forward and back, rotate and turn. The train almost lulled me to sleep—once I was curled up on two seats next to each other, another time stuck in an overheated car with someone's head on my shoulder—I wanted so badly to fall asleep, to just let the train slide me to West Oakland or Glen Park and let me waste away and vanish and melt in the sun. I wanted it, I wanted it, I wanted it, but I could not want it enough, and of course then I had to call in sick to work that day and ride BART again until night fell.

CHAPTER 11

Series 3: Correspondence
Subseries A: Personal Correspondence

Dear Sol,

It's me, your future self.

You went home to the archives, hating yourself, moving slowly because you were tired and because your limbs had once again stiffened, lost the marvelous elasticity Elsie's blood had given you. You moved slowly all the way down in the elevator, and into the archives' door you shuffled like an old man.

I remember how you tried to cry. I remember how restless you were, sitting first on your sofa and then on the piano stool, and then on the floor. And I remember how alone you felt, totally alone for the first time in your life, you who had always preferred to be alone anyway, and yet who had no idea what it meant. I remember how close you came to killing yourself that night, and how strange it is that you went from ecstasy to misery that way, but that's how it is with you, Sol, that's how it always will be: you freeze your feelings until you can't, and then when you thaw, you thaw with such heat of shame that you melt and evaporate.

Not that there wasn't real shame in what you did, but can't you see that there's some amount of grace in the world, some amount of forgiveness for people who want something that's strange, but that they are given permission to take? Not a lot of forgiveness, and it depends on the permission and the wanting and the taking, but still a certain amount, for God's sake. The two of you agreed to do it, and now because someone beat you— Elsie is going to tell you it was a queer-bashing, but she's wrong, you were beaten for attempted manslaughter, for reckless driving—you're going to beat yourself.

I know something you don't know, Sol, but it's not something I can tell you, nor something I can name. It would be valueless if I tried to hand it to you now—yes, valueless and without weight, not a gold ring nor the silk shawl that can pass through it, but the shawl is a more accurate metaphor. I know how not to hate myself for what I am, but still to be aware of how I could hurt people. I know how to do them at the same time, just as you knew how to do both, but not together. And I can never convey this to you, I can never break it over your head, I can only leave you to weep at last, in the reading room, where you have tried to distract yourself by working on the

CHAPTER 12

Alcohol, Morphine, or Idealism

Elsie emailed me in late morning:

Hello, lover ;)

I found something HORRIBLE. Do you remember the old Claytime bulletin board, before there was even the AOL group? SOL, WE KNEW EACH OTHER THERE. At least, I think this other person is you, but I feel like—the piano, the last name, the fandom—who else could it be? (Ann Persand, obviously, is me.)

I almost don't want to send this to you, because I'm so nasty to you in this exchange, but looking back at it now, it seems so delicious, such a good sweet fruit, to know that I've actually known you all this time. It makes me imagine us as teens in love, which I think you'll agree would have been AWFUL.

More seriously, though—I can't know this without telling you, and I do want to talk it over if you read this, and especially if you remember it. Let's talk soon? I love to hear your voice.

* * *

From: rsk1977@aol.com (Ruth Katz)
Newsgroups: alt.fan.feetofclay
Subject: Slash reasons
Message-ID: <1995May24.205783.5438@aol.com>
Date: Tue, 24 May 1994 17:31:11 GMT

I have written slash for two years. I don't really have time for a hobby, since I go to school full-time but I'm also a musician (piano) and I have to spend most of my free time practicing. I only have time to write during lunch at school. I just put a PBJ in my locker and write in a notebook with my other hand. Most of my stories stay in the notebook unless they are really good. Two times I have actually transcribed my stories and put them here: "The Long and Winding Road" and "Love Under the Gun" (lemon). But generally I want to keep my standards high, so I only post the ones I think are good enough to be professional work.

What I want to know is why I do it. I'm a lesbian, and yet my only fantasies are about men. I only write Shalk/Zaduk or sometimes Zaduk/Shalk. And in this very busy, regimented existence in which I live . . . why do I spend so much time with my notebook and pen, writing in an empty classroom about two men wandering the streets of an empty city, hiding from monsters and furtively kissing when they can? What it is is, it feels real to me. It feels more real than my real life . . . not in a crazy way, because I can tell the difference between reality and fiction, but because the emotions give me a thrill that's deeper than other thrills, and shoots through all of them, like being stabbed in the gut with a very sharp knife. I love playing the piano. People think my parents forced me into it, but nothing calms me down like playing does. At the same time, nothing THRILLS me like that hour of my day that's devoted to slash, slash, and more slash. I know normal teenagers are supposed to be thinking about sex all the time, but I don't. I was surprised by the one time I wrote a sex scene. It just came out of me. I didn't imagine it beforehand or anything. I feel like maybe the part of me that's supposed to be thinking about sex all the time is thinking about these sad men in love. Their embraces feel more real than any embrace I could really have.

Rant over . . . I don't know what the point is . . . I just wanted to say something about it. I'm not sure I want to know why I do it. People tell me it's like how straight men enjoy lesbian porn, but if it were like that, then there would be lesbian romance novels, and men would like them.

* * *

From: ANNPERSAND@prodigy.net (Ann Persand)
Newsgroups: alt.fan.feetofclay
Subject: re: Slash reasons
Message-ID: <1994May25.535498.5543@prodigy.net>
Date: Wed, 25 May 1994 16:12:05 GMT

First off, there are lesbian romance novels, Ruth. Have you heard of DESERT OF THE HEART (made into the film DESERT HEARTS), or THE PRICE OF SALT, or the BEEBO BRINKER books by Ann Bannon? These were re-released in the early eighties, and I've found copies of all of them in an ordinary used bookstore. All very good books.

I'm bisexual myself, and I think gay and bisexual women are just drawn to slash because they are hungry for any gay stories. There aren't many stories out there about women loving each other, and sometimes those stories just feel so intense, so distant, so impossible. I might love women, but I'm never going to go on a road trip with the rich woman who picked me up at my 1960s department store job; I might love women, but I'll never be a brilliant and glamorous English professor hooking up with my landlady's wild daughter on the divorce ranch. These things feel totally out of my reach. In some ways, stories about men being together seem less impossible, maybe because those men aren't on a divorce ranch or fleeing a husband with an unlikely name; they're piped right into my living room. I do sometimes watch two men who seem very close on television, like Zaduk and Shalk for example, and feel a special kind of warm thrill of the kind that you mean. Not a thrill of the body, but of the spirit, because it reminds me that gay, lesbian, and bisexual people can love each other. Maybe it's that lesbian pulp novels were supposed to all have sad endings, although none of the ones I've suggested above do. Without a story that happens on screen, there's no ending, so without making the gayness explicit, there's no need to lose hope.

I guess I also feel a powerful call to write slash and read it. But I don't. I write stories about women instead. It's hard, because the instinct is not there in the same way. These stories aren't comforting. They don't just pour from my imagination like the gay stories do. They're hard to write. We aren't given many tools for imagining women in love. I don't know how to use the tools I am given. But I think I owe it to myself and my sisters like you to write pairings between women, to show women being hurt and comforting each other, to show women working to make a better world for other women. I think I understand why you write what you do, but I think you're going about it wrong, and I think you should reconsider before you get too set in your ways.

* * *

From: rsk1977@aol.com (Ruth Katz)
Newsgroups: alt.fan.feetofclay
Subject: re: Slash reasons
Message-ID: <1994May26.348347.3538@aol.com>
Date: Thu, 26 May 1994 15:02:16 GMT

I guess my question is, why would I want to read lesbian romance novels? I may be a woman, but I don't like women that much, sometimes. I don't know why. I think there's nothing about us that makes us worse than men, obviously. That is so obvious that it's not worth saying. I consider myself exactly like a man, except that my body's different. I know I'm smarter than almost all the guys I know.

And there's nothing about how women behave that seems like a problem to me. They behave in all kinds of different ways. But when you say I should read and write lesbian stories, I don't know, I'm repelled by the idea. What do these women from the sixties have to do with me?

When I first came into fandom, someone told me that order matters when describing a pairing (Zaduk/Shalk = Zaduk is the top). I don't think everybody does it this way, but I do. I don't know. I just like to imagine the two of them falling in love, over and over and over. It's never enough for me. They were brought up to mistrust each other, but they realize that they have to trust each other to get through this ordeal, and something in that is more powerful to me than whatever about college professors and landlady's daughters. Does a thing have to be bad just because it's easy? Can't I just do something because it comforts and thrills me? I don't have a lot of things that do that for me, Ann. My music helps, but it doesn't make new things. It just makes things go away. If women are here to create, is it so bad if what I want to create isn't women?

I understand what you mean about it being important to change before you get set in your ways. I think about that a lot. It often feels to me as if I need to make every decision very carefully or I'll get on the wrong path and it will be impossible to work my way back again. Different paths of light streaking off into the distance, but each one is only one, and if I take one, all the others will go out. Do you ever feel that way?

* * *

From: ANNPERSAND@prodigy.net (Ann Persand)
Newsgroups: alt.fan.feetofclay
Subject: re: Slash reasons
Message-ID: <1994May26.436538.4537@prodigy.net>
Date: Thu, 26 May 1994 17:37:25 GMT

Yes, I often do. Sylvia Plath writes about this excellently in *The Bell Jar* (not a lesbian book, but sometimes it feels like one to me). The metaphor she chooses is fruit on a tree, and the different fruits rotting before she can touch them (wife fruit, famous author fruit, professor fruit). She can only pick one, and the others will rot. I feel nobody understands how teenagers actually feel. What is it about getting older that makes people forget what it was like to be young?

In answer to your question, I know what you mean, but yes, I do think it's wrong to make things just because they're easy. It's so EASY to imagine Zaduk and Shalk falling in love, because we've been brought up to feel that men's stories are more important and interesting than women's stories—so two men in love is twice as interesting, and two women in love isn't interesting or important at all. It doesn't feel easy or fun to write Kate/Sarrine, and sometimes that's really depressing to me, because it makes me recognize how much I've been brainwashed. But I also think that you can't make something you're not living. I will say that again. YOU CAN'T MAKE SOMETHING YOU'RE NOT LIVING. (I am not shouting at you; I would italicize that if I could.) We shouldn't be writing about people we can never be, and we'll never be men. We won't get them right. We won't serve ourselves. We won't serve other women. It would be fun, but self-destructive, like an addiction. I do deeply feel like reading slash is a drug, and the only thing to do is quit. I'll close with a quote: "Every form of addiction is bad, no matter whether the narcotic be alcohol, morphine or idealism."—Carl Jung

In the reading room, I had begun going through Tracy's correspondence. I found it quick and stylish, much-repeated though the best lines were; at last, I began to understand her appeal. Tracy wasn't a wit, but she was quick—fast, but also like the quick of a nail, sedimentary and bitten-down, someone who could see to the pink roots of things. You could see it when she wrote to Elsie (and Ali) that:

Your body has become necessary to me—by which I don't mean that your mind is not, but it's the body, the body, the body that relationships are built on, and I don't think I understood that until I met you. I learn it again and again with every lover I ever have, and I also don't understand it at all until I meet each new lover who is going to be really important to me, and you are really important to me. I think you are my last lover. It is so strange that in our lives of searching for love, if we're monogamous, we are de facto looking for our last lover, the person we'll have our last orgasm with. We want to know how our lives will turn out, we want to know the ending, and we use love's augury to do that. We tell our future in our lovers' entrails.

But I don't want to talk about what's within you. I want to talk about your body, and how I need it. I need it to tell me the shape of my own. I need you as I need my hands; I need you because I need my hands; I need you because my hands need work. I need the parting of your thighs because my mouth needs work. You are for passion, and you are for comfort, and I want to roll around with you in a great big bed until we're old and it's finally over.

When Elsie called, I said, "I've been reading your love letters."

"Not *mine*. She never kept mine." I heard the soft susurrus of sheets and closed my eyes. "How are you, Sol?"

"I got beaten up last night."

"What? Who?"

I told her about the meeting and about Jim, and she interrupted me with a series of staccato sounds that somehow couldn't stop me from telling all of it, right there, until the end. She finally flagged me down with, "Sol, this isn't right. You have to go to the police."

"Like fucking hell is a trans vampire going to the police."

"You got queer-bashed."

"He was right. I could've killed you."

"You could not," she said. "You're not dead."

"I am, though."

"I would remember if I fucked a corpse that night."

"I don't think you can imagine what it's like to never see the sun again. Until it's happened to you, it's—it's just theoretical."

"But, Sol," she said. "Sol. It didn't happen. Look, this was fucking dumb of me. It's not the first time a horny person ever did something dumb. I won't ask for it again. And I'll take it up with my therapist. But you have to let go of what *could* have happened. Nothing about what *could* have happened meant you deserved to be beaten up by the facilitator of a fucking support group. I'm sorry for my language. It's not you I'm mad at."

"But if it had happened, I would have deserved it."

"You would have deserved love and support. Either way. That's what I want for you. Even if I'm not the person to give it—"

"Do you think you're not?" I felt my voice high and hot against my hard palate.

"No. I mean. I think I am *a* person to give it." Her voice was high now too, and faltering. "I really am sorry about what happened in bed. I don't think you could completely control yourself."

"I couldn't. It was—" I wiped at my eyes with the collar of my T-shirt. "I never saw a therapist. I probably should've."

"What about for transitioning?"

"It's informed consent," I said. "I'm good at seeming more together than I am. Or, Christ, I used to be."

"Me too. I wouldn't usually do this kind of bonkers shit. It just felt so good to feel something. I haven't felt much of anything in years. Even before she died." A hitch in her voice, a hiccup. "I'm sorry, Tracy."

"For what?"

"She deserved someone better."

"She deserved love and support. Like you said. And I know you gave her that."

"Look, can I see you tonight? Here?"

"Yes," I said. "I'll take a rideshare. I'll come as soon as it's dark."

"'Come'? Do you want to risk leaving me that kind of opening, Sol?"

"I mean, we're having this big talk about risk."

She laughed, and then said more soberly, "I wish I'd done better by you. And this is what *did* happen. I figured out your old name and Googled it. And I showed you that message board crap. Shitty timing."

"Yeah," I said. "Apology accepted. It sucked. But, counterpoint: you also showed me how embarrassing you were as a teenager."

"I was terrible," she said. "And I still am."

"I mean, I'm still that kid too. Pretentious little linguistic magpie, takes strangers' advice like I just met an angel in a movie."

"Oh, Sol, you're so much more than that. You're sweet and clever and good in the sack, and you have that tooth gap."

"Was that—like, intentional faint praise?"

"You underestimate what a tooth gap is to me. Look, I'm the one who's still a kid. I have no job and no life. I wouldn't even be on the AO3 board if I didn't give them all kinds of money. I sit in here, I watch TV, and I feel bad."

"Those are my hobbies too."

She sighed a little laugh. "You're lovely, Sol. I wish I could just have a fling with you and keep things light and fun, but neither of us really does light and fun, do we?"

"I don't think so. I do heavy and sad. I'm a piano player, not a trumpeter."

"I don't think I could fuck a trumpeter."

"You'll fuck a vampire, but not a trumpeter?"

"You can't ask me to hold myself to this."

"That's what she said."

"I know what I said, Sol," she said, and hung up.

The ride to Marin was long and I went to sleep again during it, only waking up when the car began to soften and rock over a bed of cold gravel. The driver hadn't said anything the whole time, the surest sign that I was being gendered right, although as a silhouette in the backseat of a car and with my deep voice, I nearly always pass in cabs. Nonetheless, I got out with my most guttural "Thanks," reflexively pulled out my phone as he rolled away, and saw that there was no service.

The house was mostly glass. The planes of it looked icy in the winter dark, as if it were a patch of cold road that could kill you. I stumbled up the uneven stairs in my unisex Keds and knocked at the door.

Elsie answered it right away, as if she'd been standing behind it. She was wearing jeans and a flannel, old clothes that didn't really fit—too-tight pants and a too-loose shirt. Tracy's clothes, I assumed. She looked tired, and her little nose poked out of a puffy face. I gave her a hug, not a kiss, and a hesitant one at that.

"You smell good," she said into my hair.

"Oh, thank you. I don't think I've taken a shower or anything lately."

"You smell like—vinegar."

"Oh, God, that's decaying film."

"But fancy vinegar. The kind they make from champagne." She took a deeper sniff of my hair. "Yes—light smell. Not like decay."

"It's called vinegar syndrome," I said. "The acetate breaks down, and the smell is acetic acid. I don't know why, but everything in Tracy's collection seems to break down faster than it should. Did you find that was true?"

"Oh. Yeah. But I just thought—this house, it isn't insulated well." She gestured vaguely around her. "Sometimes I found something really weird, though. Like, a kind of sap would build up—"

"We've seen that too."

"Shit, I'm sorry. I thought I got rid of all of it."

I shrugged. "Can I sit down by the fire?"

There was a gas fire burning somewhere off to my left, up a flight of carpeted steps that floated out from the wall. Everything in the house was thickly carpeted; it was too dark to see the color. It smelled like 1000 Roses lotion with a thin overlay of damp. I have no idea how she'd detected the acidic smell on me.

"Sure," she said. "But I had a surprise for you. I'm not sure if I should keep it a surprise—because it might also freak you out."

"What is it?"

"I rigged the lights outside so that when I turn them on, it looks sort of like the sun's out. Do you actually want to see that, or would it just scare you?"

"Elsie, that's . . ." I hesitated. "It's interesting. That should be interesting."

"Okay. Then sit down by the fire like you said, and I'll give it a shot. Can I bring you a drink?"

"I'm okay, thank you."

I sat on the sofa—a shiny reddish brown velvet, like the coat of a horse. The fireplace was white brick, and all around me I was aware of those black windows, not so much like glossy ice now as like melting ice, condensation streaking their insides.

Despite its orange flames, the fireplace was cold and so was the room. Elsie must have been working hard and physically not to be cold there.

Then the floodlights went on. They were sore-bright, the kind of white that slips into the soft space behind the eyeball and explodes there—nothing like daylight at all. I jolted, but not for the reasons that had worried Elsie. The shadows along my body, along my clothes, pooled like heavy ink. They drew and redrew themselves over me in quick curves like lightning. I got up, crossed my arms and felt my fingertips biting into my elbows, looked out the window, but all I could see were the three bright studio lights, staring at me like curious monsters in a certain kind of scary-cute film.

Then the lights went out, the show was over, and the fire was once again the only light in the room until a quick soft kiss of dimmer lamps appeared, revealing built-in bookshelves, a display of Emmy Awards, flash photographs of women at evening parties. The appearance of the lights outside had been like a flash too, a long, slow, heavy moment before the eye or the shutter could close.

"That didn't work at all," said Elsie, but there was a bit of the old husk in her voice, a wry humor that seemed to scan and examine the situation like a computer, which I had not heard since before our movie date. "But you have to admit, it was a little bit like the sun."

"Though I walk through the Uncanny Valley," I said, and relaxed a little myself.

I put my arm around her and pulled her close to my side, feeling her strong fingertips palpating my arm.

"How tall are you?"

"Five-seven," she said.

"It's a nice height. I can put my head on your shoulder."

"You know," and by now I knew that when Elsie said "you know," she was about to say something I didn't know, "before I met you, I sort of imagined that trans men would be different."

"Yeah?"

"Like, really, *really* butch. And like the only people who would do it would be the ones who were . . . tall. I didn't realize you could just do it. I mean, you must not have an easy time being small, but you did it, and I bet you're happier."

"I'm capable of happiness," I said, "is I guess how I'd put it."

"How did you figure it out?"

"I barely remember that anymore," I said. "You know how it is when you're hiding something big from yourself, and then you stop, and you can't imagine how things used to be. I know it happened when I quit music. I know I had a breakdown around that time. It wasn't as dramatic as it sounds—I think people imagine classical musicians sort of like they imagine chess players, like when they snap, they start seeing crosswalks as piano keys, and the wires of the suspension bridges as guitar strings, and they dive into traffic or off the bridge—but I was depressed like I'd never been before. I don't know what it was, but I couldn't get up and do lessons. I pretended I wasn't home. I stayed in bed and pretended I was reading, and I pretended that reading was what I needed. And that's when this thought started to curl around my heart and squeeze. It wasn't a new thought. It was a very old one, I think, except that instead of being about a sort of general unhappiness that I knew was my fate, I wondered if after all I could be happy. And I began to wonder if all of these things—my inability to have sex and my trying to put it all into my work and then work falling apart, and losing the ability to concentrate or feel anything—might actually be related to the vague feelings about my gender that for ten years I'd been telling anyone who would listen. And then, when I actually started transitioning—I tried hormones without telling anyone—and it was ecstasy. Before I even looked any different, I *felt* different. My body felt *beautiful*, and I felt like I filled my skin all the way, instead of just ninety percent of the way, with the rest all air. And I'm still not happy, but I know I could be. If I hadn't gotten to be a guy, I think I would have just given up on all this a few years ago. Instead it feels like there's something about life to remember. Does that answer your question?"

"I think I feel like that," said Elsie almost faintly. "I think I feel sort of like that."

"Yeah?"

"I know it sounds—I mean, look at me. Look at what I wear. But I was thinking after we hung up about—how do I be a person? And some very small part of me said, maybe that's how to be a person."

"Tell me more."

"I know that people like me—the way I am. I know I look good and people like to fuck me. But being with you before, I only really felt alive when your teeth were in me. And I want to feel alive some other way. And I want you to help me."

I stilled, and put my hand on her knee. She was breathing fast. I felt as if this confidence were something very hot that she was placing in my heart with tongs.

"How can I help?"

"I don't know." In her throat I felt her heart speeding up. Her voice was coming out in a whisper, tongue and jaw pulled back. "But how *could* I? I have this *body*. I have this whole body. I have all these clothes."

"So you think you might be a boy."

"Or like I'm maybe not a girl. I don't feel like a man at all. I've always liked women best. Always been a feminist. But this body sometimes is just too much for me. Piloting around inside this body. I've told Tracy this, when we were drunk, and she said she felt that way too, and she thinks everybody does."

"Elsie, let me just ask you this. Is there *one* thing I can do to help right now? One thing, no matter how little. A way of touching your shoulder." Underneath, a live-wire feeling: the terror of whether this had, somehow, been my influence and my idea.

"I want you to be with me like you'd be with a guy. Treat me like one. I don't know. Have you ever been with a man?"

"Not *been*, as such. I've kissed them."

"How did you kiss them?"

"It wasn't since I was a teenager. And how do teenagers kiss? It's supposed to be great, kissing people when you're fifteen, but I think mostly everyone's greasy and goofy-smelling, inside and out." I sighed. She was looking down at me with the softest eyes, lightly ringed with water.

"I haven't even kissed a lot of people."

"Nor have I."

"What about the girl you hired to give you sex lessons?"

"Oh, we didn't cover kissing."

"Did you really think of it that way?"

"Well," I said, "yes. I mean, I mostly wanted to learn how to, um, get a woman off. I felt embarrassed not knowing what to do with my whole body—"

"You paid someone to let you get her off, and *you* didn't get off?"

"I didn't want anyone to touch me," I said. "I still like to get off without anyone touching me."

"But—we definitely touched before."

"'Me' is a euphemism," I said.

"*Are* you a euphemism?" She lightly fingered the side of my jaw. "You seem solid enough to me."

I closed my eyes. "No. Like I said. I feel like I missed all the important turns in my life. I'm over forty somehow and I've done very little."

"You were a concert pianist."

"Which means I've done very little. Look, Elsie, should I— can I just kiss you?"

"I wish you would."

So I kissed her, and I tried to make it the way I'd have kissed a man, grippy and tentative, as if we had equal strength. Held the elbow, not the wrist or around the waist. Elsie slipped four fingers into my hair, raked it back, closed her velvety eyelids. We sat there forehead to forehead, embarrassed, nervous, not knowing what to do next. There was woman everywhere I looked. I could not pretend that I was kissing a man, not with the way the faint down on her cheeks stirred under my nose, with the way her hardening nipples pressed against my chest. I couldn't tell you about Elsie's breasts without becoming pain-fully trite, but if you could put your head in my head and could *feel* the light touch, the way they shivered, the blue veins, you'd know what lushness is.

And I'd never cared for guys. I've been with so few people anyway, and guys were always being thrown onto me, pushed against me, when I was young—a needle to be halted with noth-ing more than surface tension. I didn't like them and I didn't trust their bodies, which overwhelmed mine, threw my small-ness and breadth of hip into a silhouette relief. Their bodies could do whatever they wanted to my body, anything it struck them to do. I cupped Elsie's chin in my hand, guided her lips closer to mine. Tried to fall into it.

"It's okay if it doesn't work," she said, her hands tight around my wrists. "Sol, I want you no matter what. I want you so bad. I've wanted you since last time."

"Keep your promise."

"I'll drink from *you*," she said, and then I felt her lips nibbling at my neck, isolating one of the veins there; I squirmed against her hip. The nibble became a hard suck, and that made me squirm more, and pant a little, at the pressure and the little airless vacuum her mouth made. Then she had each fist tight around one of my hands, around the fingers, and was kissing the tops, and I thought of how she'd described my hands, *smooth and slick.*

"Wait," I said. "You should bind your chest. That'll help."

"Baby, how do I do that?" Her voice was a murmur, a purr, and I pushed my body toward her involuntarily.

"You're not helping."

She pulled away. "How do I bind it?"

"You don't have a compression vest, or anything like that?"

"No—"

"A sports bra—"

"I don't do sports. Oh, wait. Um—Tracy had one."

She separated from me and got up, and left me sitting there for a long time, the seam of my jeans rubbing against me, while I tried to watch the fire. When she came back she was wearing men's boxer briefs and a clean white T-shirt, and the matter of her chest was flattened underneath—I brushed my hand across it and felt tight polyester. Her legs were shaved, but as I hitched myself up on the couch on my knees, and caught her knee between my own, I caught a layer of sharp stubble. Instinctively, I dragged my hand up her leg, touched her face, and she copied me, and both of us imagined the two sensations merged.

"Is that nice?"

"That's really nice." Her face loosened. "I can barely breathe in this thing."

"How's it feel?"

"It's not helping me forget I have tits. How do I look?"

I touched her shoulder through the armhole of the T-shirt: warm, muscular. "Delicious."

The word came from nowhere, and we both giggled at it a little, me the cartoon vampire, she the cartoon victim. I said, "But really, you look wonderful."

"*Do* I?"

"Such strong shoulders," I said, and my lisp came out more than usual, and I retreated into myself a little. "Are you wearing Tracy's things?"

"Yeah. I'm sorry, it's all I've got."

"No, I always had a crush on her. It's fine."

"You're such a beautiful boy," she said soberly, caressing my face. "Especially turned on. Your face can't flush, not now, but your eyes burn so softly. I really turn you on, looking like this?"

"You can't not turn me on," I said.

"Then how about now?" And she tumbled me back onto the arm of the sofa, burying her face in my chest, soft clean arms in the T-shirt snaking their way up the back of my sweater.

"Uh-huh." I felt my legs wrapping around her body. "What else?"

Her hand slid between my thighs, and I was suddenly,

brutally wet. I don't always like to be wet, it reminds me of what I've got and what I've not got, but here, with her, in this living room straight out of 1995, it only felt right—it felt like hardness and pre-cum. I pushed and ground hard against her arm, and I moaned. "Oh, God, do you do bicep curls or something? How have I never noticed how strong you are?"

"Yoga. Can I unzip you?"

"Have you got a vibrator?"

"Obviously I have a vibrator, I'm a lesbian widow."

"You want to go get it and unzip me and put it between us?"

"Uh-huh." She kissed me full and hard on the mouth, and I panted and bucked against her arm. Then she was gone, and I was tonguing my upper lip, trying to keep the feeling going, until she came back with it—a big bullet, a fancy one made of silicone.

As she slipped it into her underwear, she whispered, "Really treat me like a man."

"I will. Is it going to stay put?"

The bulge was hard and lopsided, obviously artificial, but he said softly, "Oh, oh, I like that so much."

"Get it over here."

Then he was on top of me with the vibrator buzzing between us, and I had my arms tight around his cotton back, feeling the hard flattened chest and the warm shoulders above me. The long back, ass in the red briefs, and hair that from here looked like a man's long hair—the fantasy didn't need to get more advanced than that; we were panting together with the vibrator between us, and I thought in a crazy dissolving second that *here I was, having lesbian sex with a man*, and then I came, shatteringly. It took Elsie longer, and I felt him losing concentration, losing the moment, in my arms. In his ear I whispered, "You're a beautiful boy too," and I felt a gasp and a wave of emotion, palpable in the body, and I held him close, tight, and kissed him hard. When he was still, I reached delicately in and withdrew the still-buzzing vibrator, touching the curve of his hip and the hard muscle under it, and I was no longer sure what I was reaching for, or who.

We had a shower together, and I watched as Elsie bowed her head under the hot stream of water. I poured shampoo into my palm and tenderly worked some of it into her scalp; she leaned against me, her whole body shaking a little.

"That was good," I said, still rubbing the shampoo into her hair.

"Sol, thank you."

"Shh."

"That was so good, and I don't know what to do about it."

"Don't have to do anything now. Don't have to do anything, ever."

"This will ruin my life."

"Elsie, you don't have to do anything." I kissed her cheek and rinsed the shampoo from her hair. "But for what it's worth—I'm pretty sure that when every transmasc sees his chest bound

the first time—the first thing he says is, 'Oh, shit.' Oh, shit, because what's he going to do now that he knows he likes it? He
can't pretend he doesn't anymore. I don't know if that's you. It
sure was me."

"This is truly full-service archiving, you know."

"What's really wild is that I do this for every donor. You
want to lie down for a little bit? I'll have to go home in a few
hours, but I can call the Lyft, then—"

"I'll drive you, I'll drive you. I'm not scared."

"Then get some rest."

We lay in the flannel sheets of the marital sleigh bed, the scent of
musty lavender, with an ancient beige white noise machine in
the doorway. I didn't sleep, but Elsie did, brief but deep, an underwater trench of slumber. I let her rest until a couple of hours
before dawn, and then coughed and rolled over until she woke
up on her own. We got in the car under the stars and I shut my
eyes as my heated seat warmed up.

Elsie drove a nice car, an old-man car, a high-end Mercedes that
made the road seem soft beneath us. There was no light in the
sky, and no stars—a moonless and cloudy night, a soft plug
over the sky to keep it safe for me. We didn't talk much.

"Help me stay awake, Sol."

"Okay. What do you want to talk about?"

"Tell me about your work," she'd say, or "tell me about piano"—big vague questions, too big to bite a piece off of or to melt with your tongue. I'd try to tell her about collections or pieces I liked, until I realized she wasn't paying any attention to me. Still, I talked, just to make sounds. I took pleasure in the animal heat of the seats, feeling their artificial warmth under me, the way my heartbeat was like a bubble underwater.

It was only when we began to come into the city, and I was growing a little alarmed because it was only a half hour till first light (I have an app on my phone that told me about this, Vep), that she finally said again, "That was *really* good."

"Yeah, it was hot as hell."

"But more than that, it was good. It made me feel—strong, and loving, like there were big important things rolling around inside me. And I just want to say this out loud."

"I'm glad. Whether it's just tonight or whether it means anything, it sounds like it was good for you."

"Sol?"

"Yes, Elsie?"

"Are we ever going to talk about the bulletin board?"

"Nothing to talk about," I said. "It was 1994. I'm not mad."

"*I'm* mad, though, I'm mad at myself."

"You were back then too."

"I didn't even make sense."

"The individual sentences made sense," I said. "It's just all together that they didn't."

"Do you remember it?"

"Every word," I said. "I remember every word. I even stopped writing slash after that."

"But you're not *mad*?"

"It would be different if you got me to stop playing piano."

"But it's so obvious now—you were writing these characters to figure your gender out, and—"

"I wouldn't have figured it out that way," I said. "You might've even helped. It's not always helpful to do that kind of palliative care. Work that helps you stay dissociated. I'm mostly just sorry that you seemed so miserable."

"And pretentious!"

"Yes, well. I don't exactly like you now because of your peasant simplicity."

"Really? You *like* that I'm pretentious?"

"I really do," I said. "And I liked you for it then. You seemed wise as hell."

"I can't get over how I was that well read. I had no idea I'd read Plath and Bannon and Highsmith when I was that young. I thought I read them—at first—in college, maybe. That's when I remember reading *The Bell Jar*. I reread that last year. It still slaps."

"Yeah. I read it years ago, but I do recall it slapped."

"Teenagers are so weird."

"Well, you said it yourself. They're in constant crisis, and people think it's funny."

"And there's so much that seems very serious and important, and nobody will guide you to find out what is and isn't."

"Yeah," I said. "Like—it seemed so important to post under my real name. I thought I should be *honest*, and anybody who went by a name they'd made up themselves wasn't *honest*. It was so ferociously hard to use my name, and that felt like virtue."

"And they talk like drunks," said Elsie. "Very correct, trying very hard to seem normal. Obviously the mind is there, but you're being so careful that you sound like a broken robot."

"It's true." I settled back in the car. "I'm surprised you didn't get into how slash is wrong because it's against authorial intent."

"Nah. I knew what Tracy intended."

"Or whether it's wrong to portray two straight actors doing gay stuff. It was 1994. People said things like that."

"They did, but even then— Oh, shit!"

The brakes were less gentle than the rest of the car; they snapped my body forward and back like a rubber band. Halfway down the off-ramp, the traffic was simply stopped—no forward motion, a traffic jam before rush hour, in a darkness that was beginning to threaten, beginning to stir. Dread drifted down over me like a black silk scarf, a dread I had not let myself feel, or had noticed without noticing. I let out a bleat and fumbled at the door handle, but the child lock was on.

"What are you doing?"

"First light is way too soon for this, Elsie."

"Fuck. Fuck!" She slammed the horn but got only answering horns. She turned to me. "Can you get in the trunk?"

"Not dark enough. The sun has to be sealed out."

"Can you run to work?"

"It's forty minutes' walk from here."

"Fuck. There must have been an accident. I'm sorry."

"No time to be sorry. The Metreon."

"Is the Metreon dark enough? The whole wall is glass. There's the Target, the—the bathroom at the Target—"

"Not dark enough. Get me into one of the theaters. The door will open and shut but those hallways never see daylight. I don't know what else I could do. BART all day, I've done that, but it's even farther."

"Hush, then, you've got to move." She finally figured out how to get the child lock disengaged, and I got out of the car and ran without stopping, without waiting to see if she was behind me, all the way down the ramp and past Moscone Center and up to the Metreon.

The park at this hour was dewy and dark. Normally it would be lit artificially almost to the point of daylight, but tonight it was flat black. My vague plan had been to go through the Starbucks, but it was closed, and without a backup plan I was just about to run on to Montgomery BART when I heard Elsie pound up behind me. It was her heavy running tread, rubber hitting earth, and I didn't even need to turn around and look, but I did anyway, like a reverse Orpheus rescued by Eurydice.

Because it was in that instant that I fell in love with Elsie, arrested midstride with both feet above the ground, tire iron in hand like a furious statue. Wise men say only fools rush in. Elsie broke the door of the mall, mirrored glass shattering,

and there was no alarm, or a silent one. I slipped into the building as if sucked into it, already knowing I'd soon be safe,
because even behind these big windows first light would be
slower in here. I found the escalators, which during the day
were soaked in light as if they were the Visible Man's bones,
but I pounded up them and was safe, and I slipped past the
popcorn booths and up and into a theater, and I stumbled and
fell full-length on the carpeted stairs, but I was safe, safe, safe.
I felt Elsie's body tumble down onto mine, and we were sweaty
and giggling, even I was sweaty, warm with Elsie's warmth and
rosy with her too. I buried my nose in the fur of her hair.

She sat with me in the utter darkness of the last row. My eyes
rejoiced in the blackness. Elsie smelled warm and clean. We
held each other in the cold. I said, "Did you abandon the car?"

"I ran around yelling and sticking a handful of bills into different cars until one of the passengers agreed to drive it somewhere and leave it for me."

"What did you *say?*"

"I said I needed to get my vampire boyfriend to shelter. Oh,
the fourth car did it. You're not a very fast runner, or I think
you'd have gone on to BART."

"I'm a slow runner and I kept stumbling in the dark," I said.
"Then when I got to the park I was just paralyzed. It was so
dark, and the grass was black. I can't believe we just ran up
here. I can't believe nobody stopped us, there was no alarm."

"And listen. It's all silent." She raised her arm; I felt the pack of muscle in it move. "No air moving. The place is dead as doomsday."

"Is this just how it is at night?" I stood up, looked into the dark from the middle of the dark, felt the air all around me like the charcoal that artists use to make pictures of night, with only my feet contacting anything.

"Well, who'd want to break into the Metreon? Who'd ever want to *be* in the Metreon?"

"I do, Elsie, I like it."

Then a flare of light bit into the darkness and illuminated the rows and the screen with a faint outline, like scum on water. I uttered a surprisingly deep little "Ah" of surprise, and Elsie said, "I'm sorry. I'm looking at my phone. It's a power outage."

"Oh!"

The light flickered off, and the glow that had stubbled her chin and mouth was gone. We sat and stood there for a while in the dark, and then I settled back onto the recliner next to her.

"That's why the traffic jam," said Elsie finally.

"What I should do," I said, "is figure out how to get in the projection booth. Nobody will be up there, it's all digital. I can just hide out there all day."

"There's not, like, an outfit you can wear? Like an opaque plastic suit. For the sun. Someone would have to help you, of course, or you could learn to use a cane or a dog, like a blind person. But you could at least get from cellar to cellar."

"I can still feel it through plastic," I said. "I can feel it through cardboard—for a while I was still living in my old apartment, going home in the middle of the night, and I had heavy card-board on the windows. I could feel it boiling through, like sun-light shining through bone."

"C'mon." I felt her hand moving up and down my arm. "C'mon, let's get you to the booth."

All the doors in the building must have had electronic locks; they fell open for Elsie like rotten things. She gave me updates via text. First she scouted the hallway, said it was pitch, or any-way had just the ambient lights of the parts of the city that weren't blacked out, but my phone said it was first light fifteen minutes ago, so I refused. Then she came back, and I heard her before I saw her, shuffling, munching from a box of candy. The light lit up the phone again and I heard, "Fuck. Jesus. It's right back *here*."

The door swung open and let me up two flights of stairs to the booth, which was dark and musty, colder than the rest of the theater, sealed as an empty ventricle in the heart, a vein full of air. The only thing in there was the digital projector. I sat down on the dusty carpet and she said, "Do you want me to stay with you?"

"For now. For the beginning."

I was drained and shaky with the falling adrenaline, and I wanted a body next to mine. She sat down with her back to the wall, and I rested my head in her lap. She stroked my hair, there among the pillows and blankets of dust; it comforted me, that dust, because it told me that no one ever came up here unless the projector broke. Her fingers traced my skull softly, slowly. The dark soothed me like lotion.

"Oh, it's no use," she said. "I can't even sit with you like this without getting at least a little bit worked up."

"Can you tell me something?"

"What?"

"What is it you see in me?" I sat up and took her hot hand. It flexed against mine, gripping it more securely. "I don't think I'm good-looking at all."

"Your jaw," she said. "You have an incredible jawline, exactly like a nineties movie actor."

"Hilary Swank?"

"Leo. Or Clea DuVall."

"I absolutely patterned my hair after Clea in *Cheerleader*."

"I know. I love your hair too." I felt warm breath against my ear, damp breath, and then a light bite to the lobe. "Dark and smooth, but not glossy; like coal. And you'll never lose it, I guess, not now?"

"Yeah. And that was becoming a worry."

"Besides that, I love your hips."

"Oh, I *hate* my hips."

"I thought you might. But most men are so narrow and flat, and have no curves in their ass and thighs, just bony bullshit, and whoever decided that that was supposed to be good-looking? Like a man's supposed to be shaped like a lollipop."

"Or a sunflower."

"Right, and who wouldn't want to bang a sentient sunflower? That dry, ridgy stem, those big dead-looking leaves,
that drooping head. I just came right here."

She pulled me onto her lap. I didn't resist.

"This is all happening so fast," she told me.

"I know. Nothing like this has ever happened to me before."

"But you seem to know what to do."

"It's more like we're dancing," I said. "And you're a really
good follow, and I'm an inexperienced lead, but you make me
look good."

"Do you dance, Sol?"

"Not like I play. Oh!"

Her hand had crept up the back of my shirt. We giggled. It
was slow and easy, and felt voluntary in a way that it hadn't
before—there had been a desperation in us, in my office and in
her house, though now I think they were different kinds of desperation, and the thing we were desperate for wasn't each other.

"Sol, let me pay you some attention."

"You've already paid me a lot."

"But let me really top you. I know you don't like to be
touched, but—"

"I mean—I trust you. It's starting to feel different—"

"You always skip to—me."

"I'm sorry."

"It's not bad," she said. "But sometimes—I don't know." And

she withdrew from me a little. "You should see the faces you make. Like, one of those photo projects you see on Twitter, 'This artist captured the faces of twenty people seeing Elsie's tits for the first time.'"

"Is that bad?"

"It's not bad. I mean, like—anyone would like being looked at with the gobsmacked expression that people do. I know pretty well that if I'm your type—"

"Sure."

"And I think, how would you even come back from this? If I wanted—you know, Sol, when I was younger, I was really flat. I was never ultra-skinny, but I didn't get the curves till my mid-twenties. Like a second puberty. And back then I used to sort of imagine that I would go someday to a city that I'd never seen and I would live this astonishing life. I would wear a tuxedo one day and a ball gown the next and all that crap."

"Is it crap?"

"It was when I said it. And then the curves came and I felt like—okay, Elsie, you're not going to look good in a tuxedo. But I still loved it when I'd, like, tell someone my name was Elsie and they wrote, 'LC,' like the initials. Like, you see me, you see this dyketude that nobody else is picking up on anymore, because it's all buried in here."

"Buried?"

"In here," she said, and took my wrist and guided it to her chest. I closed my eyes and rocked forward against her thigh.

"Is this the control group?" I murmured.

"*What?*"

"Is this like the control of the experiment you did last night?"

"Yes."

"What are the results so far?"

"Well, they're more dramatic with regard to you than me." She slid her hands up under my shirt and lifted it over my head, and I felt her lips' faint touch against my nipple, and I sighed, arching my back against her, feeling the dry rasp of hair against hand.

"But really," she added, "it's a beautiful body. The scars—" and there was a tongue against them, and while I normally hate the wire-in-skin feeling of someone touching the half-repaired nerves of my chest, this was a good touch, a fine and careful touch. A gentle warm hand on the fuzzy small of my back, and then I was lying on the floor, and she was undoing my jeans button.

"This good?"

"Uh-huh."

"Do you want me to suck you? Is that good?"

"Uh-huh. But—none of the stuff around it—"

"Nn." The touch of her lips and tongue was careful and loving, and I thought I felt lipstick—the cool cream of lipstick— and when I came, my hips tried to buck and move, but she kept them still with two firm hands. Now I was really sleepy, and there was a sense of warmth although I could not be warm. We cuddled into each other, and I pulled her head to my chest and locked my arms through hers.

I've been saying "her," although that's a pronoun we rarely use anymore; although neither of our bodies, after a few more years of testosterone and time, is entirely like the bodies that came together in that little room.

These days, the best word for my partner is *genderfluid*, and their pronouns shift from day to day—mostly "they," but sometimes "he" or "she." We actually keep a whiteboard on the fridge about it. On the top half, they write "she," "he," "they," or something else; on the bottom half, I wrote "he" once and then never erased it. Eventually, the joke wore off, and we erased my "he" and used the space for the grocery list, but you can still see it underneath the potatoes and cherry jam.

Sometimes, on a "she" week, we still call them Elsie, though on a "they" or "he" week we say something else. And they remain "she" in all my memories of the time before. "I change pronouns when I have to," as they put it. "I was a he last week, and I was a she for forty years, and none of them are less real than the others."

It's been peculiar for me, getting used to this. I'm terribly binary myself, and hate even being *asked* my pronouns. Not all trans people are interested in being gender revolutionaries; I'd prefer to be known for my tight processing and sophisticated scope notes. I'd feel strangled by someone reminiscing about

Ruth and *she*, just as I don't want people to see my old publicity photos from the thirty seconds when I was playing piano with orchestras—skinny calves in sheer stockings, long skirts, and square-heeled shoes. I'm Sol, and now even my mother will say, "Sol, when he was a little boy."

But nostalgia's funny. I'm nostalgic for that person in the publicity photos, who would come out onstage in a long satin skirt that swished around his knees, carefully sprayed with anti-static spray. He was proud of his shiny hair and his tiny waist, because they represented a kind of success. Nostalgia is different from a good memory.

We went to sleep until the theater roared to a vicious lion of life, a whirling light tornado of life, around ten o'clock. It was a Monday and the film was *Bohemian Rhapsody*.

I listened to the movie twice before I bothered to watch it— from the rear seats of the theater, after blocking the door's lock with a bit of cardboard. By then Elsie had gone; all that was left in the room was boom and boredom, and I'd let her go and drive home in the daylight. I watched the film, and then I watched it again from sheer inertia. Between the third and fourth showings, my sluggish brain realized it was a workday and I was AWOL, and I dimly recognized that there would be consequences for it, but what the damn, what the fuck, what the hell, I had hundreds of hours of vacation time built up. I sent an email and had done with it. Between the fourth and final shows, I got a reply back.

Sol,

We have already put you down as a no-call/no-show. Please ensure in future that the reading room is empty of processing projects before you leave for the day. I had to clear out your Tracy Britton boxes for researchers, and the table was covered in eraser shavings.

- - - - - - - - - - - - - - - -
Florence Makowski
Assistant Archivist
Historical Society of Northern California
Pronouns: she/her/hers

CHAPTER 13

The Festival of Lights

That night I took the long way home, because I was tired and dirty and I trudged through the air as if it were snow, and it felt like the best way through that kind of exhaustion was to resist it, to feel it on my skin. When I was nearly back at the building I realized I was due for my blood transfusion, and even though I had drunk blood only a few days earlier, the need for it was as thick as a sore on my arm. So I went to the clinic, not bothering to go wash up and make myself tidy.

At the clinic, I lay rather than sat in the recliner. It's a subtle distinction. They poured blood into me and I began to feel a little better—quenched and relieved, like hot sand when the tide comes in, and as numb as sand too. My eyes kept closing. I barely need to sleep, but I had not slept properly now in so long; I even dreamed. I dreamed of a man who has been imprisoned and neglected until he is only a skeleton with skin over him. The surface of the skin is rough and broken, like dough. In the dream, I am trying to help and rescue the man, but although he shifts and breathes, I know I am only hurting him, making him worse, hastening his end. I floated to the surface of sleep two hours later, and felt myself filled with my private battery acid again. Equilibrium.

"Mr. Katz?"

It was Ari, the nurse at the clinic who usually works Mondays, my favorite day. I had always suspected Ari was trans; he has a youthful, earnest air, a scrubby beard which he can't stop growing, and a hairline that looks scooped away by machine. He lowered his voice, although there was no one else in the other recliners, and said, "Can I talk to you a minute?"

"Uh-huh."

"There were a couple of irregularities in your blood draw for this week. Mixed types. Now, either we made a mistake last week, or you went to a different clinic halfway through the week, or you have live blood in your system from a person. Type O, which we don't usually give here—"

"Because it's the universal donor, and it's too good of blood for me."

"It's blood that people can use whose bodies aren't adapted like yours," said Ari, looking disappointed. "You know that."

"I do."

"Anyway, it's not my place to tell anyone, but I want you to know we can tell, in case the next nurse isn't—"

"*As forgiving as I am.*"

"Buddy, don't be that way. Do you regret it?" He perched at the edge of one of the other recliners. "That's a real question. I'm really not going to tell anybody."

"It's a crime."

"It's not my place to judge that either. I lend T to my friends all the time, and that's a crime, but it's ethically right." A trans man, then. I relaxed a little in my seat, wondered how long it had been since I'd knowingly talked to another of us. Besides Elsie, maybe, but I couldn't quite get my brain there right now, tonight.

"I do regret it."

"What happened between then and now?"

"I got beat up for it. But that didn't change my mind. I just realized people can't *really* know the meaning of the risk unless they get sick, and then it's too late. It's not like my friend—who asked me to bite them—wasn't in their right mind or wasn't able to decide, but that they'll never make the decision with complete information."

"I take it your own vampirism wasn't a risk you took on purpose?"

"I was a tetanus case."

"Meta Dinius," said Ari, "has a lot to answer for."

"Her name sounds like a pun, but it's not."

"Do you wish someone had asked you?"

"It wouldn't have meant anything. Like I said."

"So—no?"

"Yes," I said. "Even so, I wish someone had asked me. So I could have blamed myself."

Ari smiled faintly and said, "Transition's like that too. You can't know whether you want it until you've felt it. But in transition's case, at least you can try hormones or binding and then step back if you change your mind. I wish more people understood that—that it's not an on/off thing. They think it's The Surgery, and then you come back in a different outfit."

"Yeah. And pretty much nobody changes their mind."

"We mostly want it more than we let ourselves want it," said Ari. I was familiar with every beat of this conversation—it's the kind of gentle check-in that trans people do for each other sometimes, this reminder that *I have felt as you do.*

"The blood was like that too," I said, and I felt the muscles of my face harden and shrink with the emotion. "Nothing I'd done had felt so right since I started T. My body craved real blood—it wanted to be alive. It wanted the thunder of blood in my ears. This is like eating paste." I touched my chest, with the bright red IV crawling into the port. "And it's so much harder to know I can't do it again, now that I know what it's like."

"I think that's usually how it is. Like loving and losing."

"*I'm* in love," I said.

"Oh, yeah?" His little face brightened. "With your friend you bit?"

"Uh-huh."

"What are they like?"

"That's the thing. You see, I've never been in love before, Ari." Those names, Ari and Sol—what is it about Jewish trans men that we all have to reach back to our roots, as if they are the only source of nourishment we have left?

"Yeah? How old are you?"

"Over forty. But it's taken me this long. And what I've learned—what's unexpected—is that with real love, you don't want the person to change. At least, not for now. Maybe the end is different from the beginning. But I can see how Elsie is a really annoying person. I don't mean it like that—I don't mean it in a crude way. She's self-absorbed, she fetishizes me shamelessly in all sorts of ways. But I see those things at a remove. The way you're supposed to see your desires, if you're a very serious Buddhist. I see them, they're obvious, but they do not *prick* me. They don't touch me at all. They're like the breezes from the fronds of plants, moving across my face as I walk outside—in the sun. I only want her to be happy. I only want her to be well. Or them or him."

"Elsie's in a little bit of a gender state?"

"We do find each other." I stirred myself on the gray velour recliner, trying to get up, to pull the IV out of the port. "Can you unhook me?"

"Sure," he said, and helped me up too, and gave me a hug. It was tight and unexpected, nonjudgmental and kind; Ari dispensed it as he might dispense a pill. "You're doing good, man. You're doing so good."

"I'm filthy, I'm homeless, and I'm fucking up at work, and I have nowhere to go during the day if I lose my job. I'm fucked. I'm absolutely fucked."

"But you're doing good. You're able to think of other people, even right now. You've got it." He let go of me, sensing maybe that the platitude wasn't flying, and said, "Want to sit with me in my office for one second?"

His office was a little booth behind glass at one end of the hall. To my surprise, there was a squat menorah burning in there, a real one with real flames and a handful of candles burned most of the way down. I sat down in a plastic chair and he sat down on a fuzzy desk chair, and positioned the candelabra a little farther away from me on his desk.

"I lit it quite a while after sundown," he said. "I light it at work so I can see it, and 'cause I have OCD and I can't handle lighting the candles at home and then blowing them out."

"It's nice." The candles were softly reflected in the plexiglass window, the wax wet, and there was an appealing halo around it from the scratches in the plexi.

"Were you a Hanukkah kid or a full English Judaism kid?"

"I was a Hanukkah kid only. Jewish dad."

"Jewish mom, but not like—I don't know, my name made me invisible even if my mom technically made me 'Jewish,' and we barely did anything. My name before was something really white, and my last name literally *is* White." The candles flickered against his pink face. "Whereas your name sounds like what a movie star from the thirties changes his name *from*. Or a cartoonist."

"Krazy Katz."

"Yeah."

"Well," I said, "a long time ago, our people got caught in traffic on their way back home from their girlfriend's house. The power was out all over town, so what they did was, they broke into a movie theater—"

"Oh, I saw the board over the door!"

"And by a miracle, there was no opposition to the Maccabees as they broke into the theater, and by a miracle, there were five showings of *Bohemian Rhapsody* when none had been paid for—"

"And by a miracle, there was enough oil to upgrade to a large popcorn for only fifty cents more?"

"I'm trans, dude, I produce miraculous amounts of oil *all* the time."

"Fuck!" He laughed, a laugh with real brass and presence in it, and then someone came in the front door, an older man in thick gray sweats who was dragging himself forward. Ari disappeared into the room with the three recliners, and was there for so long that the candles burned down and I became aware in their gunpowder scent that I smelled memorably bad, and I wanted to go home. When I got up, Ari was just returning, and we made "gotta go" and "y'know" sounds at each other, and he told me, "Let's talk more next time. I'm here Mondays."

"Thank you so much."

"I'll be looking out for you," he said, and I left.

I wandered around the city a little before going home. I wanted to lose myself a little, disappear into a small place. I had been too much exposed to myself these past few days, and, tired though I was and worn through, I wasn't ready yet to be alone with my thoughts again. What I really wanted to do, I found to my surprise, was play piano—not play the keyboard, but go to a place with a real piano and play it *loud*. But San Francisco, though a city that famously possesses all the charm of the next world, is short on late-night piano karaoke venues, so I went back down to the archives, showered in the gym, and sat down to watch *Feet of Clay*.

I watched the finale. *Clay* ends abruptly. Tracy always said she'd planned a seven-season run, but what they got was four, and not even all of four, due to a writers' strike that left only Tracy in the room to produce anything. As a result, the last five episodes of the show feel manic, with cheap effects reflecting a life-support budget whose plug has already been pulled. I knew now that Tracy hadn't had the money to end the story the way she really wanted to, the way she did in her book:

Shalk visited Kate every few months and then every year. He never warned her and he never outstayed his welcome or pushed the bounds of what she asked him for. They sat on the flat rock and ate things from tins with knives, and he would speak of the worlds he'd seen: the cold rims of gas giants, their costly rings, the flares of distant suns, the quiet life of primordial planets which could not be touched—muddy gray life that dampened in the dark, or snotty, bloody life that burbled in ponds.

Shalk had let go, with some relief, the worry that he loved her. For him love was a matter of taking orders, and she gave him none.

They grew old between the visits, weakened in the knees, developed an anxious tendency to stumble over the rough ground and to spend a little more time resting, a little more time in sleeping bags with the wind biting at their clothes before they woke each morning in camp; a little more time simply sitting in the cabin, not at all past speech, but too tired to fashion the tricks of speech they needed to convey their feelings. They were both people of complex feelings and slow talk, and so they sat with their mouths closed and working a little, as if each was making a pearl. Sometimes he would at least play for her, hands moving about his viola in the long abstract motions that sometimes felt only tenuously connected to the sound coming out. He missed Zaduk; he knew she missed Sarrine; they could not substitute for the lost ones, but they could make the sounds of their ghosts.

Kate's clothes wore out periodically, and he supplemented them with his—cozy things with drawstrings. As the last years ran out, however, she went back to her old uniform, saying that it was more comfortable, being made for her body and very old and soft. The effect was of a reversion to the mean. In the last year she greeted him in the full kit, with the tarnished epaulet and the bright plastic buttons and the honor cord whose decorated tip contained a poison pill. Over the right shoulder of her coat and the right half of her face, splatter-edged and vivid, was a mass of red clay.

"What's this?" he asked, touching her cheek, warm and pink with the effort of breath and blood.

"What's what?" she asked him brusquely.

"This. This clay."

"Is that a metaphor?" she asked him lightly.

"This clay, Kate. This, on your face."

She touched it, looking with amused wonder at him, and said, "There's nothing there, Shalk."

He tried to believe her. In the long years since his detective life had ended, Shalk had learned to take pleasure in believing people, and here they were, he said/she said, 50/50, two sides straining at the same big coin. He saw the mask of clay; he tasted it when he took her face in his hands and kissed her cheek—tasted it dank and sweet—and he smelled it, when she slept and he lay in his cot across the room, covers thrown aside, trying to toast his cold body in the heavy heat of the fire. Once, at its edge, he saw something whitish, naked and reflective, that he knew to be bone. But in the morning nothing had changed, and he prepared to re-turn to his ship as he had prepared many times before, after exactly forty-eight hours on the planet.

"You can always come with me, you know, if you want to."

"I thought we were past that kind of discussion," she said quietly.

"Would you like me to ask?"

"It won't make any difference. You're freezing. Here."

She shrugged off her coat; underneath she wore only trousers and a thin collared shirt, suspenders, armpit stains, a cut.

"I can't take that."

"I'm used to the cold now," she said, "and the winter is going to be mild."

"Please. I'll just be going up to the ship."

"It fits you," she said, and pulled it around his shoulders; he put his arms into it, though he could barely shove them through—it did not fit at all. It was warm and damp inside. "There."

She brushed down his shoulders and then touched them, once, lingeringly; when she took her hands away, the redness on the shoulder had wrapped itself about her hand. He kissed the hand, lingeringly, and went up into the ship.

He stayed away this time for only a week, and that was spent in orbit, worrying at himself. When he could stand it no longer, he threw the ship into reentry, ran stumbling down the stairs, into the cabin, but there was no Kate, and he had not expected there to be.

And once again, we were alone.

That was it. The miha won, and even more bleakly, I'd learned what Tracy wanted out of a marriage. For I really did believe that this was her vision of living with someone—worn and sexless as an old duvet, a hooking and a dragging down. Something in it choked me.

That night, after I finished the episode and read the end of the book like some solitary fannish god, I sat down to the online archive where Elsie had found our posts, and I looked up what I'd said. This was a few years later, when I was already on my way out of the fandom and had begun college, and I recognize myself a little less acutely.

From: rsk1977@yahoo.com (R.S. Katz)
Newsgroups: alt.fan.feetofclay
Subject: What are the miha?
Message-ID: <1998Dec20.537568.3722@yahoo.com>
Date: Sun, 20 December 1998 23:01:46 GMT

Whenever we talk about the nature of the miha, someone tells me that they're a metaphor. Fact is, I know they're a metaphor, but what for? Why do we never get beyond saying that word?

The thing is that we know so little about Trace Britton's intentions, or her life. I don't know if I'm the only one who didn't even learn till last Fall and the /TV Guide/ interview that Trace is actually a lesbian, but if I'm not, everyone else had access to a much more efficient rumor mill than me.

Trace is mysterious. A Mona Lisa of TV. She looks like a heroine from one of her own shows, with her short hair and her cocky smile. And she's created something just as inscrutable as herself, except that the miha are /supposed/ to be that way. Well, maybe she is too.

What do we know about the miha? They are clay. They want to know what it's like to be human, but they don't want to /be/ humans; they apparently despise them. Certainly they have no qualms about killing and replacing them. Does Trace identify more with the miha or the humans? Does she feel like she's pretending to be a person, and if she does, is it about curiosity or obligation?

I've tried to look at the story through a liberal or conservative lens, and it doesn't make sense for either. The miha are /sort/ of like the kind of "other" that a racist or a sexist might see. Featureless and violent. But they have absolute power, and they make you pretend, so they're also the kind of "other" that a person of color or a woman might see.

I don't know. When I watch the show, I don't think I see something political at all. I see the work of someone who, maybe, just didn't like people all that much. Who wants to like people, and wants them to have justice—that's what the character of Shalk is all about, right, justice? But also, someone who just plain doesn't like them. Who feels wounded by them. There's nothing else underneath that. It makes me think of DS9, which at least has the guts to say, "Well, the Dominion and the Cardassians are different kinds of fascists, and Bajor is a religious dictatorship, and the Federation is a better America." After a while, if you're not willing to admit what your metaphor is, you find yourself just saying nothing with it, except for what you're most afraid of.

So that's my theory. There's no metaphor.

Was I right? Pulling aside the fact that I cared about this show *so* much, or rather /so/ much, and I spoke its language deeply in a way that I never will again, and my interpretations are hazy because of it—yes, I rather think I was. I think about the sheer bloody misanthropy of the show's ending, and the different kind of misanthropy of the book's ending, in which every remaining human is dead, and I don't see anything but nihilism.

I mean, take the death of Sarrine, the most infamous lesbian TV death until Tara dies on *Buffy*. Sarrine is killed by a miha she's tried to befriend. This is Sarrine's whole deal. She imagines that if she's just kind enough, warm enough, empathetic enough, even though by nature there's not an inch of warmth in her, not an inch of warmth even to fill the soles of her feet—she can *convert* these beings that want only to crack humans' skulls and replace them, to slip into their lives.

There is a gorgeous late episode, not written by Tracy, in which Shalk meets a husband whose wife has been replaced by a miha. The husband and the children have tried to survive, as people on the show do, by pretending that everything is normal. Shalk sits down to dinner with the family, and the miha-wife—played by a very talented actress covered in layers of red latex—serves them rice and beans, and the four of them talk, the father and the child and the detective and the miha-wife, with polite pauses as the miha's lips move soundlessly. Shalk makes many errors in guessing what she's saying, which is dangerous, because the moment anyone fails to act exactly as if the person the miha replaced as alive, the miha will kill you. Shalk and Zaduk, in the end, are the last people alive on the station because they have no friends or loved ones, so the contagion of the miha doesn't reach them.

Shalk survives this scene because the father and the child are very good at pretending, and cover for all of his verbal slips, first as if they are mere rudeness, and increasingly—as Shalk begins to urgently ask if they are all right, if they are safe—as if he is acting insane. Eventually the father stands up, picks a fight with Shalk—"You won't treat my wife that way, you're treating her as if she's not here"—and Shalk apologizes to the miha-wife, and he can guess from her body language what she tells him, which is a strained "Thank you." As he leaves, the father puts his hand on the shoulder of the miha-wife, and she puts her hand on his.

The final episode steals this moment, in a repetition that felt a little nightmarish, because it had happened on the show so recently and had been so powerful to me. The miha, made of molten clay the color of olivine, snaps Sarrine's neck as she stands looking out the window in the hallway of Kate's ship. Kate comes out of the bedroom, drawn by the sound. The two of them look at each other, the miha through eyes that are no more than the vague shapes of Sarrine's sockets, Sarrine's body on the floor with her lumpy pop of gray hair spread out behind her. Then Kate reaches out, the miha reaches out, and it's not clear which of them is comforting the other, whose grief is the more powerful.

I still didn't know what to do with the book, with all of its layers and fragments, the heavy depression that seemed to press down and smother every jot and period of it. A whole box of everyone being miserable, flashbacks, flash-forwards, fragments and whirls of messy text, followed by an apocalyptic ending in which even the surviving characters from the series die, in which the miha, with their flesh of clay, are all that's left of humanity. Puppeting, parodying, going about the lives of the humans they've replaced, and more than that—the point-of-view characters of the whole business.

I don't know what do with Tracy, except to say that nothing

ever seemed to work out for her, despite her remarkable talents; that she loved badly and too often; that Elsie adored her and also openly admitted to finding her choking, exhausting, like a horse's bit; that she was unhappy, and unhappy in her body. She had told Elsie that probably everyone wanted to live another life. I don't want to simply say that Tracy was obviously a trans person, or what have you, but she had the same kind of pain that closeted people have. A pain that you don't know what to do with. Most often, it's like a migraine, a vague and yet very specific soreness that lies across the head like a streak of latex. She was aware of that pain, and she tried to articulate it over many years, many lines, many girls, but in the end, for whatever reason, she was simply unhappy in the body that killed her.

CHAPTER 14

Dead Buildings

We all know the claustrophobia of being in a dead building, that sense of being watched. We've all been in a building that has burned, or that has been abandoned for many years, or that's just been empty of tenants for too long. The context is gone, and so is the unique pressure that human breaths give to the air in a room—that sense of its being heated, flushed, slightly toxic. Instead, there's just air, swept clean, and the whiteness or the slick dark colors of the walls, and a terrible weightlessness.

If this is bad, how much worse to be surrounded by dead information. When I woke that morning, I felt it immediately. Something had changed in the night, and I was sure this something was part of the same process that had put the sap in the folders, that had made the air feel rough and shattered after Elsie and I had fucked in my office. Changed, and accelerated—critical mass, takeoff.

All around me was the voluptuous rot of dead collections. Yes, all the surface problems were there: paper separated into pulpy ash, film vinegarizing, plastic dissolving into the stiff crackle of the dry shell and the oozy plasticizer that had once made it supple and loose. But beneath that, you could sense that the information itself had cracked open and flowed away, and what it left behind had nothing to hold it together. Every object in the world is formed of molecules that have come together by human intention, and now the intention was gone, and the objects were losing their shape. When Florence walked into the archives, I was still standing there in my sweatpants and T-shirt, smelling the air like the plastinated body of a dead hound, and she froze there too. We looked at each other, our expressions identical.

We checked the climate control. We pulled open boxes. We put on N95 masks and opened canisters of film, and gasped at the smell of acid that pressed into our nostrils. Staples had dissolved into rust, newsprint into snowy brown flakes. Florence hung back as I examined the plastic pieces (binders of unprocessed papers, small toys, cellophane wrappers). It seemed safer for only my body, inviolate and almost poreless, dead itself, to touch them.

At lunchtime, she invited me up to Starbucks with her before remembering that we hated each other. Then she said, "Would you, I mean—would you like a coffee? Do you . . . drink?"

"Sometimes," I said. My arms ached. "But it's all right. You don't need to get me anything."

"All right," she said unhappily, and disappeared to the bank of elevators.

I went to my office and sat down heavily at the desk. Aware of an acrid smell, I opened my desk drawer and beheld my dick. I'd never had the chance to throw away the packer I'd left, and that Florence had seen. I quickly shut the drawer again on the half-melted, foul-smelling thing, feeling freshly ill.

That day at four thirty, Darya beckoned me over in the kitchen. I went to her feeling prepared to lie; I had had no ordinary eight hours, and the anger was seething in me like muddied surf.

"Sol," she said very quietly.

"What is it?" I asked, as calmly as I could, but the edges of my voice were made of speckled rock; they scraped against each other.

"Are you still living in your office?"

"No."

"Where are you living?"

"With my girlfriend, for now. In Marin."

"You're staying in *Marin* and coming to work every morning before dawn?"

"I don't have a lot of choices," I said. "I did everything I could to obey you, but it takes time to find a home in this city, and I can't afford to live alone."

"Fine. I'm glad to hear it."

She walked to the other side of the room, pointedly I thought, and examined some of the posters tacked to the wall. I bent to wash my hands. From behind me, I heard Darya say, "I'm glad to hear you have a girlfriend."

"Thank you."

"You've always seemed lonely, if you don't mind me saying so."

"A lonely Sol," I said. "Well, my condition is like that."

"Is she a vampire too?"

"No." I shut the water off and stood looking into the dripping sink.

"So, I've been told," she said quietly, "to take your office key."

"Told by whom?"

"Edward." The executive director, rarely seen by any of us. That way that a common name can become weird and numinous if it's attached to a dense enough local power.

"And you told Edward what, that this happened?"

"I told him about our meeting."

"You know that I can't leave the office still until after eight. What would you like me to do for the three hours after we close? Shall I stand in the hall?"

"Sol, please don't do this. Don't get like this with me. I've told you, it's not my job to solve your problems."

"It would be your job to solve my problems if I were getting harassed, or if I needed to change something with my health insurance."

"But neither of those is true. Do you have the key on you?"

"You're taking it now?"

"Florence unlocks the office every morning at eight," she said, and stood there waiting until I dug through my key chain and produced the key. I held it up and she took it from my fingers.

"Is this a prelude to anything?"

"It's not," she said carefully. "And I'm glad to hear that you're making progress towards having a place to live. How has your day been otherwise, Sol?"

"There's a crisis in the archives. A climate control problem that I don't understand. Well, it's beyond a problem. We've been finding a lot of materials that are more decayed than they ought to be."

"Really? Like the climate control has been off for a while?"

"Well, no. It hasn't. And we monitor it. Something else is wrong that we don't understand. I'm still working on it."

"You think it's something we should contact Marcelle about?"

Marcelle is the director, the one I'd been substituting for during her maternity leave. A mild, pastel sort of woman with an implacable archival mind. She'd been sending me occasional updates about her baby, but with her usual hesitancy about sharing some things with me—not as if I shouldn't know them, but as if I might find them boring, or even offensive, as a person who's infertile twice over.

I suppose I appreciate her kindness in not bringing up the baby to me. But I *like* babies. They're alarmed by my cold arms, and of course I don't meet many these days, but still, I like them. All the same, I was never one of those trans men who wanted children, though I remember trying to pretend that I did when I was young. Someone would dump a baby into my lap and I'd turn to my mother and tell her brightly, "I want one!" She was always concerned, and encouraged me to wait, as if I'd leapt to sign up for immediate impregnation, rather than shown a general interest in reproducing someday. I think my quite real lack of desire must have added lead to my words, so that my lightheartedness failed. It usually does.

CHAPTER 15

Spirit!

I didn't stand in the hall after everyone else went home. I brought my office chair with me and sat there instead. I scrolled through my phone, and I tried to read and then to call Elsie, but I couldn't get cell service. I finally opened my tarot app and drew my card of the day, which was the Sun. I broke into my gelatinous sweat and then the app crashed, the phone crashed too, and at the same time the lights went out. I put my face to my knees.

The lights came on a few moments later, and I restarted the phone, though the screen had a line across it now that I couldn't make go away. Then, miracle: a call from Elsie. An hour still until I could leave this dark and foggy place, to go up into the dark and foggy night. I had not breathed since the lights went out.

"Hello?"

"Sol?"

"Yes, it's me."

"I tried your office phone, but you weren't in. Are you out at a bar?"

"No, I'm in the hall. They took my key. It's been—a day. I'm a little overwhelmed."

I told her about it. Her voice, always curiously active even at rest—little flutters, hums, wobbles of sound, never impatient but always reactive—went still as I spoke.

"Sol, you know, there *are* solutions to this."

"I don't know what to do."

"It's not logistically impossible. You can get a room at an SRO. We can tape the windows—lots of SROs in walking distance of your work."

"You're right," I said. "We'll work on it—I mean—"

"I'll help you work on it. This isn't okay, and you need someone to help you."

"What are you the scaredest of, Elsie?" The lights in the basement flickered again. "I'm afraid of a lot of things. Fuck, I'm—I'm just afraid I've never accepted that my life is never going to be the same again. That every year, it's a little worse than the last, and not because of anything I did, but because of bad luck that makes it harder and harder to deal with things. That things are on the decline. That things are decaying. That I'm decaying. And—the lights are going on and off. I swear to God, it feels haunted here."

"Maybe it is."

"Nope, it's not."

When Elsie spoke next, there was a charge in her voice, something that smelled electric. "Sol, if something like you can exist, then why not ghosts?"

"Something like me?"

"Someone who's alive the way you're alive."

"Barely?"

"At all."

"I've stopped being grateful for the miracle of my survival, and just started living as best I can. I think that's how it is for everyone."

"That's not what I mean. It's a metaphor, it's a compliment. I mean you've done so many things with your life—"

"Oh, I see—"

"The piano, the archives, transitioning. You've done things that most people wouldn't even think could be jobs or—ways of living. Or possible. All I've done my whole adult life is think about *Feet of Clay*, and think about her. You're the first *new* idea I've thought about in twenty years. And if you were here now— I'd just crush you to me. You sound so scared."

"I am scared."

"We'll be together again soon."

"I'd like that."

"Do you want me to come now?"

"No, you don't have to—I'm still exhausted. Oh!"

The lights went out for good, and the only sound was a

trickling somewhere behind me, a juicy trickling that seemed to be inside the back of my skull. The phone was dead; I thumbed its little button and got nowhere. I stood up, and felt the chair rattling off down the hall.

"Spirit!" I don't know why I addressed it like Scrooge addresses his ghosts, or why I suddenly realized that I believed in it. The deadness of the air around me had given way to a wet life, like the life of a mossy cave. It was impossible to believe that there was nothing here but me. I felt as if the very bacteria that lined my stomach and lungs had been expelled from me in a lush carpet, and had bred to fill every wall and floor and door of the archives, every box, every tea bag in the break room. The room felt alive, and the life felt as if it were *of* my life. I coughed, and the sense grew stronger.

"Goddamn it, what do you want from me?"

The pulsing feeling of life continued, and though the air was black, I colored it in my imagination with blue and green moss, with a generous dolloped mold, with oily water that flowed sweetly down the walls. That's all decay is, after all—it's life going on. I felt empty and powerful and connected to the gross and the wet. Then the lights went on, and I was looking at the clean antiseptic basement hall of my building, blinking at the grit and sand in my eyes.

Upstairs, the air was windy and clean. It was winter, but of course I wasn't cold—my denim jacket was only cosmetic, and its enamel pins (a segment of keyboard, the universal symbol for no flash photography) unwarmed by my skin. I had put on an outfit I liked, black joggers and a black T-shirt and the jacket and a plain black baseball cap, my hair down and loose—and I walked down the street, feeling a charge of excitement at having nowhere to go. I could go to a movie now, any movie, and walk outside with the crowd into the hiss of white streetlight. I could go to a bar and drink a glass of cider. I could—I checked my phone. It was still dead.

No, not only dead; there was a crust of crisp gray lichen over it that my thumbnail couldn't remove. I went to the repair shop in the Westfield mall and had the gratification of seeing it squinted over by the owner. I left it with him, gave him my office number, and walked free into the city again. No distractions, nothing with which to fill this useless garbage bag of time, which could both stretch and break!

I left the mall and walked down Market, and at the barbershop near my work I had my hair cut, just like that, the hair I hadn't dared touch since I became a vampire. I knew this haircut would be my last. Short back and sides and a fade up the sideburns, please, and yes, something that will wear well, that will look good in ten years or twenty years, because I am planning to live a long time, yes, a very long time, ever so long, in the coffin that they say we sleep in (not a bad idea, it seals out all the light). Voilà! Vamoose! I'm tidied, and the Sol in the mirror looks older. Why didn't I do this forever ago? My hair, the wire hair of a dummy or a doll. Even corpses' hair is supposed to grow a little.

I started to come down from this jag at a Jewish deli near Civic Center, where I was shuffling at a copy of the *Bay Area Reporter* and trying to taste some pickles. Nothing to do. God, those nights. I often fantasize about the twenty-four-hour businesses you used to see in seedy films of the seventies: greasy spoon, porn theater. I took my time over the pickles and went to the library, which was open another hour. Got two Forster novels and *Watchmen*. Signed in to my email:

Dear Elsie,

I'm sorry we were cut off. My phone died, and appears to have died permanently. The power is still pretty fucked at my work, and I no longer understand what's going on, and I've reached the point where you *know* you're trying not to think about something. But I wanted to write to you.

I can't believe we've only fucked four times. I feel like I've been fucking you for years. You know most male vampires can't get it up—the blood flow isn't enough, but for me, with this little thing, the blood I have is enough. It's probably the only advantage I've derived from my association with vampirism. The other month at work I mentioned my "sun sensitivity" and someone asked me if I had lupus, and it was all I could do not to say, "Lol, no, I'm a vampire, not a werewolf." So the jokes are okay, too, if they didn't lodge in my throat.

Maybe I should be out about it. It hasn't done me much good to be closeted. But it freaks people out so much, and if I admit it, I have to start living with it. And after five years, you'd think I would have learned to live in this vampiric body, but I haven't. I guess all our bodies are vampiric, they take everything they see, and mine is only more honest about it.

You know what really drives me crazy is when people use it as a metaphor. I went out with a girl once or twice—went nowhere—soon after I got sick, and we had some kind of fight about givers and takers, you know, as mature people in their thirties do. I was supposed to be a taker, and she came out with it, with "You're not the first vampire I've ever dated, Sol." But she used my old name. She'd known me, before. It was an accident—it slipped out. Oh, I don't know what's wrong with me tonight. I love you. I love you love you love you love you love you. Love you.

It's been so long since I loved a person. I'm not sure if I ever have. I'm not sure if I even loved my mother, when I was little, the way I love you. You are so hot and fierce and strange. I hope you know, too, that if you go on with the idea of being a guy, or if you decide some other gender fits you better, fits you better than her old clothes did—because you can get your own, I know it's scary and you feel like nothing will ever fit, but you'll find your brands, and in five years it'll seem just so unlikely that these small practical matters felt so huge and impossible to get over—if you end up transitioning in any way, I will be there with you, and I will call you your name every time.

Don't worry about me even making a mistake. Your name will become that name completely. I used to know you by screen names, and I never liked you then; now I know you by a name that's equally arbitrary, was equally picked by a much younger person (I'm sure we are older, now, then our parents were when they had us?), and is equally easy to break open and escape. If you want to stay Elsie, I will be Sol with you. I don't know if it will ever make sense for us to live together, for us to make anything together, but I know it will always make sense for me to know you. And that is a comfort, that is a great ship upon which I can rest on the waters.

The library's closing pretty soon, so I will write again in the morning. Email me your number again, for when I get a new phone. I love you, love you, love you.

- - - - -
Sol

Finally I logged on to Facebook, sober and ready to move on, and ran a few searches. I had to used advanced search to find it, but finally I found it:

Vampires in the Archives!

I clicked JOIN GROUP and answered the questions ("Are you a person with vampirism?" "Do you work in archives and special collections?" "Do you agree to our community standards, including person-first language, content warnings when discussing mental health or self-harm, and no pens or liquids?"). Yes, yes, yes.

To my surprise, the group add came up just before I had to leave the computer. Without looking at the other posts, I hurriedly typed:

Hi, I'm an archivist in San Francisco and I've been a vampire about five years. We've had a strange event in which decay of archival materials has rapidly accelerated, with no obvious problems with climate control or environment etc. Electronics have also been having trouble working in the archives, including things like my phone and even the lights. To tell the truth, I'm worried that this has something to do with my presence in the archives. I was walking around there tonight—like you do—and had this acute, spooky sense that this rapid decay was part of me. Tell me this is nuts. It is really nice to meet a group of people like me who can tell me that this is nuts without telling me that I'm nuts. Take care.

CHAPTER 16

A Sense of "Deadness"

I rode BART out to the airport, just for something to do. I read *A Room with a View*:

It so happened that Lucy, who found daily life rather chaotic, entered a more solid world when she opened the piano. She was then no longer either deferential or patronizing; no longer either a rebel or a slave. The kingdom of music is not the kingdom of this world; it will accept those whom breeding and intellect and culture have alike rejected. The commonplace person begins to play, and shoots into the empyrean without effort, whilst we look up, marvelling how he has escaped us, and thinking how we could worship him and love him, would he but translate his visions into human words, and his experiences into human actions. Perhaps he cannot; certainly he does not, or does so very seldom. Lucy had done so never.

I kept getting distracted from the book by the harsh lights of the platforms or the soft lights of the apartments. But all I had was the soft and grainy reflected light of the page, and sweet Forster talking about music—and the struggle, the strain, to put music into words. The description of Beethoven's Fifth in *Howards End* is good too, but it's overstrained from the start: "a goblin walking quietly over the universe, from end to end."

It's a funny thing, but having given up music as a vocation, I find that I don't speak it as well as I used to. Since I refused the call, I cannot call back. Instead, I've come to like words, even hokey, corny words, even the dumbest and grossest grotty little jokes you can imagine. The werewolf thing. Or my secret vaudeville gag: "God misheard my very simple request, and so He made me a pianist." Even the smallest word is a prism that breaks up ideas and makes them visible to the eye.

I put the book in my lap and watched the night city go by. A long, long tracking shot. In my head I began to play another Beethoven sonata, number 32, which is what I've always imagined Lucy played in that scene. I think it's possible to "decide it should triumph," as she does. My fingers flexed under the burden of desire to play that sonata myself, right now. I ought to commit another crime, I thought, as the train pulled up to the platform and I got up to stretch. The last train was on the other platform, humming to itself. It was nearly midnight.

I ought to commit another crime and break into a place with pianos, into a theater even, and slam and slap my way through that sonata. I honestly believed I didn't need sheet music to do it; my fingers remembered, though maybe they'd simplified and brightened it a little, as they do with any memory. I got off at Civic Center and I walked around looking for a place with pianos. I found one at Pentacle Coffee, with a ratty velvet-topped bench, and hung around wondering how to get in. You can't just break every window you see. *Today* I know how to break into a building, but back then it seemed impenetrable and probably alarmed. In the end I went all the way to Berkeley to play the tuneless one they keep chained up outside the MLK building, and it turned out I did remember the thirty-second sonata, though I could barely rattle through that brutal allegro, and I forgot some of the jazzy thrills in the middle, or put them out of order.

As I rode the night bus back, I reflected on the things my hands remembered. My body is an archive. This is not a new idea; it's common enough in PTSD theory, but I always think that people who aren't archivists miss the ways that archives are quite specifically vampiric. My condition is essentially that of a dead body on life support. Archives are the same—dead information, provided with artificial blood. That was why it had been so shocking and upsetting, that day, to feel my collections *go* and know they would not be back. My body remembers old touches, even the touches of keys. It remembers what it felt like to have boys try to get inside me. It remembers so many things my mind does not, and closes and opens its muscles accordingly when something seems familiar. I am a bundle of sensations bound together by cords of memory. I thought that when I got back to work, I would find out what had happened and if it was my fault, and if it *was* my fault, I would—

What? Quit my job? Go out and see the sun? Both seemed equally impossible, equally melodramatic, and yet I would owe it to the archives to leave the scene. If there was a phone or computer where I could check Facebook—

I bought a new phone at the twenty-four-hour Walgreens in the Castro, emailed the number to Elsie, and signed in to Facebook. Of course all the vampires were online at that time, and I found a long thread in response to my question.

CHAPTER 17

Series 4: Subject Files

Frances Wood

Eidolism

Hal Vo

It's eidolism

Cadence Holder

New members please look at the other posts before you post another question about eidolism

Alice Coleman

Welcome to the group, **Sol Katz**. You might indeed find more useful information in the posts below, but to recap, because not everybody has time, "eidolism" is an in-group term we came up with to describe a phenomenon that very often happens around vampires and old things (as archivists, I think we were just in a better position to observe it than most). It's from the Greek word for ghost. We don't understand it well, and nobody outside the community has studied it, but anecdotally, it's very common and often devastating. Often it's some combination of accelerated decay and a sense of "deadness," but some people think there are other symptoms, like illness in other staff and—the one good effect—a decrease in insect activity. Usually it happens after many, many years (it happened to me before I retired as archivist at Industry College, where I had worked since 1962—yes, I'm very old!). Even if you've been at your institution for all five years, it's unusual for it to happen so quickly. Perhaps you're just more observant than some others. Hope this helps, and please stay in touch if you would like preservation or professional advice. Been vampire since 1977, back when most of us were still converted by other vampires. I have been very blessed to live this long, but perhaps because vampirism was so unknown at the time, it was less stigmatized, and my employers at Industry arranged for me to have a little basement apartment under their main auditorium, through which I could travel to the archives via an old converted steam tunnel. It's lovely, especially when the students—despite its boring name, it is a music school—have recitals over my head! I often go upstairs to hear them. I'm the phantom, as Daniel Johnston said, of my own opera. Take care!

Sol Katz

Thank you, Alice. This explains a lot for me. If I am totally honest, I have been living in the archives for several years (in my office). That's probably why. I don't even know how to process the information that this really is my fault, if only because I am what I am, and I did what I did. I'm sorry I asked an obvious question. Is there any word on what can stop eidolism, or if anything can? Obviously if Alice retired right after, that means things didn't go too well for it at Industry? I'll look at the other threads, too, sorry. I'm sorry.

Alice Coleman

Don't be sorry, Sol. No, things definitely didn't go well here at Industry! Many of the collections were saved, and we had a robust digitization initiative, perhaps more so than any other music school in America. There are a lot of computer people in City of Industry, which is exactly what it sounds like, and besides I have always tried to be forward-thinking about this, despite growing up in a time when computers ran on paper—we actually have quite a stunning punch card collection here, the Violet Mercado papers, a composer who tried to invent a music notation system using this early punch card code—if you are a musician at all, you'll find it fascinating. I have to stay away from the archives now, which is probably healthier for the culture there anyway—it's never good when a retired person hangs around after their time—but I miss my collections, and I do insist that they send me new digitized materials to redact/write metadata, when possible. Sometimes I also design Web sites for online exhibits. That's how I keep my hand in! LOL!

But please don't beat yourself up. The reason everybody asks about eidolism is because everybody who finds this group is in distress about it. And it's NOT your fault, any more than carbon dioxide was your fault, when you used to breathe. (Or do you still breathe? I have the impression you are fairly new to vampirism too, because you look like quite a young man, although perhaps it's an older photo? Mine is from 1982, but I still look exactly like this, LOL—it's just a very flattering one, and I know that the kids now use filters to get lighting like this on purpose.) It is just an effect of being around the collections, and the problem is that we generally do not get to stick around to get to the bottom of the mystery, once someone figures out it's us.

I do not know if anything can stop it! I would love to know, for so many obvious reasons. Please keep me updated on your quest. You can "friend" me here or text me. I will send you a message with my phone.

CHAPTER 18

ABABO, BAOBAB

The remains of the sleepy, effulgent mood were still with me as I rode the elevator to the basement an hour before dawn. I was still half thinking about myself as an archive, the traces of blood types moving around in my veins, the muddled words—ABABO, BAOBAB—Rh minus, Rh plus. ELSIE was in me too, ELSIE's blood, and as the elevator doors slid open I saw that blood again.

She was standing right in front of the elevator as if waiting for it, wrapped again in one of her polyester wrap dresses with the geometric pattern, both her eyes blackened and blood slicking the side of her face and the side of her neck and down into the neckline of the dress. Her eyes were wide and wet. My first thought was to catch her, although she was not falling. I said, "My God, what's happened to you?"

"I came to see you."

"What happened? Was it—"

"I got in a car accident on the highway," she said, and from her mouth came a bubble of blood that popped. "I got out and came here."

Her voice was slurred, sleepy. I caught her arm. "How did you get here?"

"I was on the bridge. I walked out of the car. I came to see you."

"Come on," I said. "We're going to the hospital."

She couldn't walk very quickly. I let her lean on me, but there was only so much I could do to keep her moving forward. I almost took a car to Saint Francis, and didn't—it was so close—and by the time we stumbled in, her body sweaty and warm and human against mine, every hot part pressing in a different way against her clothes and my body, so that I was close to tears, it was fifteen minutes until first light. The emergency room had windows. I'd like to say I felt greedy for the blood that kept pouring down, but something in me knew it was dead blood, no more use to her or me. Perhaps I'd like to say I was tempted, and resisted temptation. But I was not. There was a long line of people at check-in, and then it was just seven minutes to first light. I leaned across the desk and hissed, "I need help immediately."

"I'm sorry, sir, but there's someone behind you who's bleeding."

"This is my partner. I'm a vampire. I need to get away from those windows right now or I'll die, but I need you to tell me she's going to be safe and all right."

The woman in scrubs who sat behind the desk had eyes made up in mascara that matched the blue of the scrubs; she looked young and exhausted. She said with bizarre hesitation, "I can't guarantee that anyone will be safe and all right. Here."

She made a call on her desk phone. Behind me, I heard Elsie stumble on the linoleum and I turned and saw her try to drink the air; falling, and too heavy for me to stop her from falling. I tried to grab her arm but I only wrenched my shoulder, and probably hers too. I crammed my hand over my mouth. I couldn't go on like this. Behind me, I felt a light touch on my arm. It was a security guard.

"Come with me."

He led me to what must be the janitors' break room—in the basement, past the laundry with its hot breath of starch. The elevator doors closed at two minutes to first light and I began to shake. The guard's face was blank. My belly still hurt from being kicked at the meeting. After all of that, there was still a bruise.

CHAPTER 19

Series 3: Correspondence
Subseries B: Business Correspondence

From: Florence Makowski
To: ALL-STAFF
Re: Preservation issues

This email involves something I didn't want to talk about, but in light of the disaster that's ongoing in the archives right now, I feel like I have to. As a few of you may know, Sol Katz has been squatting in his office for the past several months, if not years. Sol is a person afflicted with vampirism and he can't safely be outside in the light, which I have sympathy for. It seems like a hard life. However, it's illegal for him to live in a commercial building, and it's DEEPLY uncomfortable for those of us who have run into him obviously in pajamas or with personal hygiene items on his desk. All of this doesn't matter very much to me; it's mostly Sol's problem to have and to solve. My real concern is with the collections.

We don't know how archives react when exposed for a long time to a person who is a vampire. We know that nobody really understands how vampires keep alive, other than that if they get timely infusions of blood, their bodies, which in a medical sense are dead, continue to function and have their decay arrested. We know that what's happening in the archives is rampant, uncontrolled decay.

We've checked, and the climate control is working fine. The humidity is fine. The air quality is normal. And yet I looked at newspaper clippings from the 2000s yesterday that look like clippings from the 1950s (and, yes, paper quality is part of it, but not all of it). I looked at plastics from the 1980s and 1990s that are warped and off-gassing beyond recognition, and to the point where they are not safe to handle. I've had nitrile gloves biodegrade on my hands while handling these plastics. It's not safe to be in the archives anymore, I'm being exposed to all kinds of deadly things, and I don't have the privilege of being a person who can't be damaged by them. I assume that Sol is out sick again today—it's possible that he's looking for a new place—but enough damage is already done. I want to talk seriously about what Sol's presence might be doing here.

I'm attaching a pdf of a peer-reviewed article about an incident at Industry College which was very similar. It doesn't mention anything about their archivist, Alice Coleman, who retired recently, but there's still a photo of her on their staff page, and she looks like a woman of about 40, while her ussearch page (which says she lives on the Industry campus) says she's 81.

Florence Makowski
Assistant Archivist
Historical Society of Northern California
Pronouns: she/her/hers

From: Marcelle Berger
To: ALL-STAFF
Re: re: Preservation issues

Thank you for your email. I am out of the office until January 4, 2019. Please direct urgent inquiries to Sol Katz,

Manuscripts Archivist and Acting Archives Director, at
sol@historynorcal.org.

Marcelle Berger
Archives Director
Historical Society of Northern California
Preferred pronouns: she or they

From: Marcelle Berger
To: ALL-STAFF
Re: re: Preservation issues

Hi, Florence. This is a lot. As you know, I'm not officially back from
maternity leave until next month, but at this point I am checking
my work email and available over the phone. I'm concerned about
the collections too.

How certain are you that Sol has been "squatting" at work? Sol, I
haven't seen any indications that anything is amiss with you, but
things may have changed while I've been gone. If so, I am concerned
about you as well. Florence, I'd like to talk to you about this on the
phone, if I can, and take the discussion offline.

Marcelle Berger
Archives Director
Historical Society of Northern California
Preferred pronouns: she or they

From: Florence Makowski
To: ALL-STAFF
Re: re: Preservation issues

I'd rather have this discussion over email, please, so that Sol can
keep up with it. Sol has admitted to both me and Darya that he's

been squatting. I don't appreciate the fact that my word is not enough.

Florence Makowski
Assistant Archivist
Historical Society of Northern California
Pronouns: she/her/hers

From: Marcelle Berger
To: ALL-STAFF
Re: re: Preservation issues

Thank you for your email. I am out of the office until January 4, 2019. Please direct urgent inquiries to Sol Katz, Manuscripts Archivist and Acting Archives Director, at sol@historynorcal.org.

Marcelle Berger
Archives Director
Historical Society of Northern California
Preferred pronouns: She or they

From: Florence Makowski
To: ALL-STAFF
Re: re: Preservation issues

Marcelle, please remove your out of office message.

Florence Makowski
Assistant Archivist
Historical Society of Northern California
Pronouns: she/her/hers

From: Marcelle Berger
To: ALL-STAFF
Re: re: Preservation issues

Thank you for your email. I am out of the office until
January 4, 2019. Please direct urgent inquiries to Sol Katz,
Manuscripts Archivist and Acting Archives Director, at
sol@historynorcal.org.

Marcelle Berger
Archives Director
Historical Society of Northern California
Preferred pronouns: she or they

From: Edward Aksimov
To: ALL-STAFF
Re: re: Preservation issues

Good morning, Florence and Marcelle. Florence, thank you for
bringing up your concerns about Sol. This is a tricky line to
walk; I don't want to minimize your concerns about Sol being
here, and how it may impinge on your own ability to feel
comfortable at work, but I'm also sensitive to how Sol may
feel about being "outed" in this way. Let's please take the
discussion offline. Darya, when you see this, please meet with
both Sol and Florence. Sol, please check in. I will also want to
speak with you.

Edward Aksimov
Executive Director
Historical Society of Northern California
"History, despite its wrenching pain, cannot be unlived, but if faced with
courage, need not be lived again."—Maya Angelou

From: Marcelle Berger
To: ALL-STAFF
Re: re: Preservation issues

Thank you for your email. I am out of the office until
January 4, 2019. Please direct urgent inquiries to Sol Katz,
Manuscripts Archivist and Acting Archives Director, at
sol@historynorcal.org.

Marcelle Berger
Archives Director
Historical Society of Northern California
Preferred pronouns: she or they

From: Darya Vlinder
To: Sol Katz
Re: Checking in

Hi, Sol, you've probably seen the email exchange on all-staff
about your living at the office. I'd like to hit pause on the
discussion until we see you again, but I'll be honest: it's harder
for me to help you when you disappear and only call in in the
midmorning. You still have meetings, donor work, and
probably processing on your schedule (come to think of it,
what you've been doing really is probably too much for one
person).

Sol, I shouldn't be writing in such detail, but I am worried about
you. Please check in.

Darya Vlinder
HR Associate
Historical Society of Northern California

From: Edward Aksimov
To: Sol Katz
Cc: Darya Vlinder
Re: Call us, please

Sol, it's been all day. Can you please give me a call at my office number?

Edward Aksimov
Executive Director
Historical Society of Northern California
"History, despite its wrenching pain, cannot be unlived, but if faced with courage, need not be lived again."—Maya Angelou

From: Florence Makowski
To: Sol Katz
Re: Sorry

Sol, I'm really sorry about what happened today. I'd contact you in some more appropriate way, but I don't know how to get ahold of you. I hope you're okay. I'm sorry I was a bitch. You have to understand that what you were doing wasn't fair to the rest of us. You can't just make the whole world yours. But I acted out of concern for the archives, for the materials, which I know you share. I really do hope you're okay.

It frustrates me that we can't be friends, because we have so much in common. We were the only two GLBTQ people in the office, among other things (or I don't know about Darya), but I always sensed that you were a kindred spirit of sorts to me in other ways.

Florence Makowski
Assistant Archivist
Historical Society of Northern California
Pronouns: she/her/hers

CHAPTER 20

Home Under Home

Even if there had been cell reception in the room, I couldn't have called. I know I couldn't write back. My eyes and mouth felt like boiled sand, heavy and dry. As it went on, I just started Googling old vampire message boards, the kind I'd tried looking at when I first got sick, and hadn't been able to look at since. Their pale brothy pastels, and the elaborate signatures with gifs of chained cartoon flowers, and the dates, 2002, 2006, had made me feel as if I'd fallen out of my proper time—as if vampirism were an affliction of 2002, 2006. Now I sought them out, like a person who feels sick and longs for a purge.

home under home [wrote edbug in 2004]. would anyone would be interested in joining together to buy a decommissioned missile site. seen them for sale for 300k-400k, but these are nice ones that have been fixed up. we could live there together and fix them up, even flip them if we were careful. totally underground safe.

Johns Hopkins Doctors Discover Miracle Treatment for Vampirism [wrote Tananda, 1998]. A team of doctors working at Johns Hopkins has discovered that heavy water (deuterium oxide) can not cure but TREAT vampirism if you are diligent in drinking it, 8 8-oz glasses per day at least, and using it in all your cooking. ALL your water intake for the rest of your life must be the heavy water. You wouldn't need transfusions and you could go outside. It seems too simple to be true but that's what they said about penicillin. Does anyone know how to get some of this?

Has anyone tried colloidal silver?? [wrote AllanJamesVitale, 2009] I've heard that colloidal silver can be very helpful for some of the satellite symptoms found in older vampires, such as the aching and swelling in the joints. Obviously it can't do anything for the basic and central problems—this isn't heavy water we're talking about—but I've been doing this for 17 years, and I could use some help with my joints and lungs.

Accident prone vampire [wrote pybie, 2005]. I am a hospital janitor and I've noticed that since I became a vampire, I am extremely accident prone. Everything seems to fall apart faster around me, and all I have to do is touch a bed or a machine for it to develop some kind of mechanical problem. It makes me feel awful, like my existence is cursed. This never used to happen. Maybe I'm just depressed cause of my condition? Maybe I'm subconsciously ruining it all? But I swear that even normal decay, and dust and dirt building up, seems to happen faster. And it's always in the more important parts of the hospital, especially the ICU. Anywhere where we lose lots of patients. Does anyone have any advice? I feel like I'm damaging everything around me just by being here. I don't want to hurt people!

re: Accident prone vampire [wrote anatasa, 2005]. Actually, I'm a sanitation worker (handle recyclables in big plant, night work), and I've noticed something similar?? Also since I changed. Never happened this way before. Crazy mold, warping of plastic. Things just arrive that way, they don't turn in my hands or anything, but it makes me feel like I am going absolutely crazy, because nobody else ever seems to open a container and have dead ants run out all over their hands. Like the world got 10% more gross.

re: Accident prone vampire [wrote sobstorie, 2005]. SAME THING. I work in a car factory and it's MY FUCKING ROBOTS. They break down SO MUCH MORE. Maintaining these things is MY WHOLE LIFE and they've just gone to SHIT on me. The oil gets thick and grainy and the code bugs out and their joints gum up like they need some COLLOIDAL SILVER!

re: Accident prone vampire [wrote pybie, 2005]. I don't know if you're dealing with the same stuff I'm dealing with in the hospital? This feels so tied to the wards where the worst things happen. It feels like it's responding to something inside me. It feels like something that feeds on death.

re: Accident prone vampire [wrote anatasa, 2005]. Dude, why would you think that?

re: Accident prone vampire [wrote pybie, 2005]. Because I do!

My phone beeped: a new text.

Hello, Sol . . . this is Alice from the Facebook group . . . just checking in. You seemed to be having a pretty bad day. How are you doing?

alice

[I wrote],

i'm reading the craziest shit on the internet

Oh, no! What is it?

it's a guy who works at the hospital

and he says they have eidolism there too

he didn't use the name, but it was obviously the same idea

and he said he "has a theory that it feeds on death"

and when someone asked why, he said "because i do"

(he's a vampire)

we don't feed on death!

blood is very alive, alice!

LOL! What a drama queen (king!). But why are you at the hospital? Are you all right?

yes

i mean it's the guy posting who works in the hospital

but i am also at the hospital actually

my partner was in a car accident

probably not seriously hurt, but i'm worried

Oh NO! I'm so sorry!

And I'm sorry my reading comprehension failed me!

I was distracted by a problem in the room!

it's ok

i'm in the only room dark enough to be safe

everyone seems to have forgotten i'm here

i'll go out in a few minutes

it's finally almost night

It's almost night here too. I'm in California too!

I do see what he means about feeding on death. Do you have the wherewithal to talk about this? I'm sorry, sometimes I get onto a topic and I forget to read the room!

that's why i texted it to you

you're good!

Well, maybe it's just because I am an archivist, and we definitely make our livelihood from people who have died (from their things). But as vampires, we do take POTENTIAL life. We live on our donors' extra blood, the blood their bodies keep for an emergency. We live on what we can beg from other beggars.

You're too young to remember this, but in the eighties, we didn't have the blood banks yet. We had to go to the hospital for our transfusions. I would sit there in the chair feeling so, so guilty, because in all the rooms around me were young men dying of AIDS.

guilty for being alive?

More or less. Some of the doctors were so afraid of the young men and what they had inside their bodies. I would hear people going in and out of the rooms so quickly that you'd think they were holding their breath inside. They were afraid of me too. Afraid of catching MY condition. The thing is that of course they weren't afraid of AIDS or vampirism, but only of different kinds of sex. Because most of us back then weren't just infected by other vampires; it was specifically during sex.

I didn't care how they spoke to me. I felt much worse for the young men, of course. It was the doctors' loss if they didn't want to know me, just because they couldn't stop themselves from trying to look through my clothes to see what I had done. (As a librarian, I was used to the public trying to look through my clothes, anyway. That sort of thing was even worse back then!) But it was exhausting, and I was always angry, and I simply didn't understand why they felt that way. It wasn't as if my condition were catching. I was hardly going to have sex with THEM! :)

I'm sorry for that terribly long text!

no, that's fine

i'm so sorry you had to go through that, alice

I've mostly been very lucky. I've been lucky to live this long.

Nobody ever thought of just deliberately giving people vampirism then. I can't believe I've lived to meet the people who got sick because of the tetanus cure.

i was

Oh, so I assumed.

Don't let me keep you from seeing your partner!

thanks, but it's not last light yet

I wouldn't know, I'm in my bunker.

The eidolism in the hospital is interesting.

a factory worker and recycling plant worker also weighed in

Vampires! Factory workers, night cabbies, archivists.

yup

You and I are so strange because we already had no-sunlight jobs.

Anyway, sometimes I really do wonder if the word isn't literally true. If it isn't literally ghosts, and the key is that the ghosts are trying to get our attention because they know we're sort of dead.

Archives are full of unfinished business. I always feel that they are haunted. Something clings to the papers after the people are gone.

we just took in this collection from a very unhappy woman

my partner's former wife, actually (long story)

i mean they were married until she died

we met later

if anyone would haunt an archives, it would be this person

I hope your partner is safe and well! Was falling in love with you a surprise for him, if I can ask? My sister came out as a Lesbian after being married to a man for twenty years, and she always said that she never knew how love was supposed to feel until she fell in love with a woman.

oh, my partner is a woman

or, well, actually, she's kind of

thinking about that, now

i'm a trans man, and sometimes people who want to date trans men realize later that they want to be trans men

but yes, I think she's always been bi

Oh, that's interesting.

People are so interesting!

I hope that doesn't read like a kind of faint praise. I just think it's interesting what people worry about and what they don't.

You and your partner seem to have fallen in love without worrying very much about gender or vampirism. Maybe I'm just assuming your mood from the way you text without capitals.

no, you're mostly right

it's last light now and I'm going to go find her.

Take care!!

CHAPTER 21

That Little Bit Inside That She Couldn't Lever Out

She was in a private room with robin's-egg-blue walls, the curtains tightly drawn although it was night. Her face had been cleaned up, though the circles around her eyes were still wet, dark, and didn't look entirely like stable ground. I sat on the bench in the window with my hands on my knees. I was glad I had the jean jacket on still.

"Don't turn a light on," she said with her eyes closed.

"I won't."

"Sol. I thought it was you."

"It's me."

"I was so worried about you. I know I'm not showing it, but I feel . . . flat. I'm not up for much."

"You were in a car accident. I wouldn't worry about it."

She shrugged a little. "I don't feel as bad as I thought I did. It felt worse worrying for years than it feels to just have a concussion now. If this was all I was afraid of—it's like I was sick all that time, and now I'm well. Like I was hurt and now I'm better. If I can do this, what else can I do?"

"I'm glad you've been able to find some meaning in it."

"Some." She opened her eyes, though in her swollen face they only opened partway. "Sol, you cut your hair."

I took off my cap and showed her, rubbing my hand over my hair to unflatten it. The fade up the sides was brisk and stubbly. "D'you like it?"

"I like it awfully much. Come and sit by me. No—sit on the edge of the bed. My face isn't contagious."

I sat up on the edge of the bed and held her hand.

"I have a question for you about my tits."

"Yeah?"

"If I didn't have them, would you still be attracted to me? Like if I was the same person, but without them."

"Yes."

"Don't just say it. You *love* them. The first time you saw me, you couldn't keep your eyes off them, Sol, do you realize?" The faint seam of a smile opened in the bruises around her mouth. "You think that if you don't make eye contact, people won't see *your* eyes either. You've got to watch it."

I felt the dim, cloudy flush—a feeling of real, productive shame—gather inside my head.

"But the first time I took them out," she went on, "that was when you were really *not okay*. You love women, Sol."

"I love *you*," I said. "I understand that now."

"And I love you too." She sighed. "God, it feels so good to say it. Your letter meant so much to me. It was a little unhinged, but so are you."

"Hinges are metal," I said. "Very prone to rust. Very bad for the materials."

"Yeah. I'm sure they are. You want to kiss me now or wait till I'm better?"

I kissed her, smelling more disinfectant and more fresh, clean skin; I closed my eyes against the sight of the bruises and tangled in her soft lips. My hand on her shoulder.

"Lower."

"You want me to feel you up in your hospital bed?"

"I want you to get me off. I feel terrible."

"Someone's going to come in."

"They gave me dinner half an hour ago. Nobody's going to be in forever."

"I'll get kicked out and won't get to see you at all."

"I could have come by now."

I kissed her face, her forehead, and I put my hand on the tender heat of her belly and slid it down into her underwear. She tensed and came to me, and I let her use my hand to get off while I kissed her languorously and felt my moist and sticky blood rise and fall. It was absurd and patently unsexy, and yet

I had never felt more attached to another person—no games, no elaboration, no quirks, just need and closeness, and two or three simple lines in each other's flesh. I didn't get off or try; it was hot and then the heat drained, and I got up to wash my hands.

"Should've done that before. We're in a hospital."

"Elsie."

"I love doing it with you. God, you're so much better than Tracy."

"*Am* I?"

"Tracy was a stone butch who seemed to fuck from a sense of obligation," said Elsie, "and I feel like . . . I did it out of a sense of obligation too. All that body mapping and trying to learn to appreciate my body and love what it could do, all that *positivity*, or I could just have been this whole time with you and just gotten off without anyone touching the parts I hate to be touched, only the ones I love to be touched."

"The skin of your face has such a lovely fuzz," I said. "Not like a peach. It has a rough tooth to it. It keeps me close. It keeps my attention."

"You'd really be okay with loving a man?"

"Elsie, maybe I wouldn't be. But I think I would be. We've tried it, and it's hot. But we just started dating, and you shouldn't decide based on what I might want, anyway."

"It just seems so lovely," she said. "You've shown me that a person can just be a boy, if you ask. I could get whatever I wanted, if I just asked. And I know there's a high price for it."

"There has been."

"I'm used to paying high prices, though. Nothing in my life has been cheap. You don't get the kind of luxury I live in for cheap. What do people do, after they've thought about it?"

"Sometimes they try on a name. Or see if they like not being called *she*."

"I'm not ready for that, I think. For now I just want to know I can."

"That's fine," I said. "I like your chest. I liked the sun too. Sometimes we give things up, for ourselves or other people. We have to give them up. Oh—you can get a real binder to make your chest flatter. That's another thing people do."

"I might do that. I like them where they are now." She shifted around in the bed a little. "They almost go in my armpits, when I lie on my back. A nice thing about getting them taken off would definitely be preventing sag. That's about where I'm at right now."

"The doublethink's real. It's because you're in a state right now where you're straddling two separate realities."

"Aren't we usually? 'I can't go on, I'll go on.' 'The test of a first-rate intelligence is the ability to hold two opposed ideas in the mind at the same time, and still retain the ability to function.'"

"It's funny," I said. "When I was a teenager, I read that Fitzgerald quote and I took it literally. I missed all the bitter irony he's using, when he's a man miserably trying and failing to get into recovery and help the mentally ill wife whose ideas he stole, telling himself his intelligence is clearly first-rate if he can be this fucked-up. I thought: *I want mine to be first-rate too. I wonder if I do that.*"

"You read *The Crack-Up* that young?"

"He's supposed to be a young man's author, except for the part where his most famous book is about turning thirty."

"Come back and sit with me."

I finally came back and sat. My eyes closed of their own accord, and her hand caressed my cheek. I said, "I found out more about what's happening in the archives," and I told her about eidolism.

When I finished she was quiet for a while. Then she said, "I always thought the boxes were haunted."

"Yeah?"

"I just didn't know what to do about it. I don't believe in ghosts. But living there for almost a year with all those boxes of Tracy—I'd wake up every morning with my lungs feeling like they'd solidified. Like I had to work to breathe. I became very clumsy all of a sudden. I dropped things in the kitchen, especially things she'd loved. We had a teapot shaped like a little white ceramic elephant. We had a crystal. Things that reminded me of her. And when I gave the boxes to you—with a perfectly clear conscience, because ghosts aren't real—I woke up excited and bold, I woke up in a good mood, with lungs as big and clear and hollow as a bottle. I woke up feeling like something could happen. And I'm sure it was mostly—I'm no longer sure that it was mostly. Because—I keep thinking it, again and again—if you can exist"—she stroked the side of my face, my chin—"why can't Tracy?"

"Why indeed?"

"The only thing about the idea of a ghost," she said, "is that Tracy was never angry. That's the one thing—she could be stressful, she could be exhausting, she was always sure that she knew what to do and how to do it, she was congenitally unfaithful—I notice you've never brought up Ali, presumably out of some sense of *delicacy*—"

"I didn't know how at first," I said. "And then it seemed beside the point."

"Well, I know all about Ali. I won because I was the one who had something inside that Tracy couldn't reach, I think."

"That'll do it."

"It's obvious," she said, and sank her head deeper into the pillow, eyes bright in the purpled sockets, nudging herself just a little to the left, to the right. "That little bit inside that she couldn't lever out. But never violently. I mean, she just wanted to make a girl moan until she got the final moan in her hand that meant she had you, the innermost petal. And I would have, if I could. But I couldn't. She was never angry. She was never vindictive. She wasn't even complicated. She was just a very simple butch, tall, hot, a silver fox—"

"Foxes are more of a transmasculine trope."

"So I can't call her a silver fox?"

"Silver wolf."

"A big husky dog. Siberian husky. With blue eyes." Elsie

closed her eyes. "I really am concussed, baby, and I need my rest. It's been perfect talking to you. What are you going to do now?"

"I don't know. Walk. I need to send an email or two."

"That sounds awful. You can stay in my room if you like."

"I'd rather not," I said. "I'll just distract you from your rest."

"Probably true."

"I keep thinking about what you said," I said, putting on my ball cap. "If I can exist, why can't ghosts be real. And it makes sense. There's so unbelievably little that anybody knows about my body. Trans bodies or vampire bodies. It's such a small population, and none of us have any money. Do you think I know if I'm prone to heart attacks at the same rate a cis man is? Or why we get cramps?"

"Cramps?"

I sighed. "I'm telling you, for real, cramps with orgasm is a transmasc thing. Very common after a year or two on hormones. You just fold up with them. Sometimes they go away, sometimes you need to get a hysterectomy. And nobody knows why! And nobody's asked! And it's not even on the medical radar, even though it really affects lots of guys' quality of life, and is invalidating and embarrassing and keeps us from wanting to come. Anyway, that's your information minute for tonight. Sleep well, darling. I love you a lot."

"'Darling'?"

"I'm practicing for when I'm an old Jewish man." I paused, hand on the door handle, and looked out over the bed and the dark and the view of the city, and then I left.

CHAPTER 22

A Very Bad Liar

Dear Florence,

Thank you for your emails today. I haven't been able to reply to anything I've received—a small family crisis, I'm sorry—but I gather that if I had, I'd have learned that I've been fired. I won't pretend I didn't bring all this on myself. I can't quite agree that I deserve it, insofar as anybody deserves anything, but I do think you've been right about me the whole time. I have tried to live by making my work my life. It has made me step on people—in small and big ways—who just use work as work, and I've tried to valorize it, as if I care more about the archives than other people do.

No, this wasn't going to work. Who cared?

Dear Florence,

I understand that I have been fired, although I wasn't in to hear it happen. What you have to understand is,

Also a nonstarter.

Dear Florence,

You have taken away something I loved more than I have ever loved anything before

Dear Florence,

I am sorry, I am sorry, I am most heartily sorry for my very great fault.

Dear Florence,

I saw the email chain today. I assume that what it adds up to is that I'm fired. I wish you hadn't exposed and outed me in these ways. You had no right to do that. I wish you had been more sympathetic to the difficulties I have conducting my life. I also realize, though, that since I have a job and am making decent money, I did have options besides living at work. If it wasn't possible in a practical way, I could have asked for advice. If it wasn't possible in a psychological way, I could have asked for treatment. My life is difficult, but there are vampires who truly have no options, and I'm not one of them. And you're right that it would be hard to come back from the awkwardness of seeing some of the things you've seen. You didn't come to work to find family or to live with someone. You just come to work to work.

Instead of solving my problems, I tried to make an impossible situation work by lying, and I am a very bad liar, except to myself. I am sorry.

I also may have a suggestion to make to you. I have been doing my own research into what my presence in the archives may have been doing to collections. I believe that the collections themselves are also a factor—not that I should have been living among them, irreparably damaging the very thing I treasured most, but that there is also an exacerbating factor, something that's not understood yet. If you are open to discussing it with me—and I understand why you might not be—I will be available at [my new number] in the evenings. I will also come to work soon to collect my things, but I will have to arrange a night pickup, probably with Darya. Once again, I am sorry, I am sincerely sorry, and I know that without me, there would be nothing to exacerbate.

Solomon Katz

She called me almost immediately afterward, as I was still sitting in the Starbucks in Union Square, drinking a quadruple-shot mocha that tasted to me like a mild milk chocolate, and which almost succeeded in giving me a buzz. I had been listening to the *Emperor* concerto, probably my favorite piano Beethoven (I often speak as if there is only one composer for piano, and I'll tell anyone who asks: that is true).

"It's Florence."

"I know."

"I don't know why I'm calling you."

"But you are."

"What's your theory?"

"Well," I said. "You know how a collection will just seize on you sometimes. You'll be going through it, and suddenly, despite your best efforts at professionalism, you'll be overcome by a sadness or just a frustration with life. You know what I mean—an unprocessed collection, maybe one that's sat for a long time. The letters still folded in their envelopes, maybe never opened. The sophomoric essays that still say so much about what made a person anxious and who they wanted to be. The magazines someone faithfully kept, and you know they're worthless, but they thought they were so important—important enough to throw out to posterity like a farmer sowing grain. God, the futility."

"I try not to think like that."

"I don't try hard enough, which is why you still have a job and I don't. Do you ever feel as if processing those collections sets them, somehow, at rest?"

"It sets *me* at rest. Sol, I'm still trying to break into this profession. I don't have the energy for mysticism about it."

"I blame the Tracy Britton Papers," I said, "and I want to finish processing them, and I want you to consider helping me."

"I shouldn't have called you, Sol. Good night." And she hung up.

CHAPTER 23

A Storage Unit

I spent that night wandering around the city. In the morning, at the office, Florence wasn't there. I told Darya I would pick up my things in a week, and she told me, "You'll bring them home today."

I said, like an obedient stormtrooper in *Star Wars*, "I'll bring them home today."

So I rented a storage unit in SoMa, bought some boxes and a big handcart, threw my keyboard and all my effects into it, and moved it to the unit. I spent the rest of the day in storage myself, after realizing the big door was at least as sun-tight as a screening room at the Metreon. I slept the night on top of the boxes, under the unplugged electric blanket. And then Florence called again.

"Hello?"

"It's Florence."

"What time is it?"

"It's the middle of the afternoon. I'm upstairs on the street."

"Yeah?"

"So I don't believe in ghosts."

"No."

"But I do believe in . . ." Florence hesitated. "Vibes. Okay. There's a *vibe* in the archives, I thought it was the tension between us, but it's still there now that you're gone. And I thought more about processing, and what it does for me. Separating all the rotting newsprint and putting it in an acid-free folder. Straightening out all the papers and putting them in another acid-free folder. Removing the rusty staples. It's like . . . taking care of an animal. Like pulling something sharp out of a dog's paw. And when you label them all, and you describe them, and you look back at them at the end of the day, you do feel like something is . . . tamed. Like you trained a dog to be a seeing-eye dog. You taught it a job. Now, instead of being a snarl, or a mess that makes everybody miserable, you've made something that has a purpose again. Even if the purpose is just to teach people."

"I used to be a teacher," I said. "I disagree that it's a 'just.'"

"Okay, fine, but it feels that way. These things can go into the vault for years after that, and never get looked at. But sometimes someone does look, and they get something out of it. And sometimes, when you process, you see something in the collection that makes it rougher, not smoother. Uglier, not prettier.

You learn someone was a real Nazi or that they spoke really, really cruelly to people they love. But at least you know." Suddenly her voice was labored with emotion. "At least you finally know, and you can move on. That's a kind of closure too. And right now those Britton papers are just sitting in the conference room, and they're probably just going to go back into the vault as is, because nobody but you thinks it's that important to preserve drafts by someone who made *Xena*."

"It was *Feet of Clay*. Florence, where were you in the nineties?"

"The *closet*. And I don't know why, but it all makes me unbearably sad."

"Me the fuck too."

"Do you think that you and I could do it in a weekend? And then I'll move them to the vault, never admit they're already processed. Someone will find out eventually, but by then everyone will have half forgotten this. Do you think we could make this sad dead lady happy, if we did that?"

"I actually do," I said. "But don't just do this because you regret helping get me fired. You acted according to your principles and I did fuck up."

"You're a really good archivist, Sol. I want to remember you that way."

"Doing what I loved most."

"My only question is, if the answer to exorcising a ghost is as simple as processing the collection, why is this a problem anywhere?"

"What archives in the world has ever not had backlog? Most

of the ones I've known have been *mostly* backlog. It's that simple, Florence, it's the confluence of three things. How little
people know about vampires, how little they know about archives, and how little they know about the undiscovered coun-
try from whose bourn no traveler returns."

"How did you figure this out all of a sudden?"

"You figured most of it out too. I talked to a lot of people
and I sort of synthesized what they told me and then I had an
answer that made sense, or almost-sense, or at least the damn
collection is going to get done. I love that collection, Florence.
I've never wanted one more."

"Even though it's got so much trash?"

"I don't want to be high-handed about this, but we won't
know for fifty or a hundred years if it's trash. Let's get it organized and go from there."

"Sol, where are you going to go?"

"I don't know. But it's not your problem, so please, try not to
worry about it."

I visited Elsie in the hospital again on Friday evening, but we
said nothing of moment. Her face looked drier and cleaner,
even with the bruises at their peak. The blood stayed where it
was, just below the surface.

Then, Friday night, I met Florence in the familiar basement.
I felt nervous, keyed up, as if I were on a date or about to do
some complicated solo sport—like gymnastics, which everyone

wants you to do when you're small and look like a girl. I avoided gymnastics, but not gynecomastia. A few little jumps up and down in the hallway, and then the lights plunged to black. I lit up my phone's flashlight and saw the stairwell door open, and Florence emerged from it, in black pants and a black T-shirt and a black ball cap and a denim jacket, same queer uniform as me.

"Did you do this on purpose?" I called out to her, and she squinted into the light and said, "Do what?"

The lights came on, revealing what I was wearing, and she laughed a little in shock and relief. "No. You used to be a really cute lesbian, Sol."

"What am I now?"

"A guy. Why were you standing here with the lights out?"

"They did that by themselves." I pointed meaningfully to the locked archives door. "We'd better get started."

CHAPTER 24

Processing

I'd missed just losing myself in processing. I brought something to archives that most archivists don't have, but all professional musicians do—an endless capacity for boredom, great golden wheat-smelling fields of boredom above which I fly like a man in a hang glider. I can always find the quirk, the little shift in scent, that makes *this* iteration interesting and unique. But for a long time, I hadn't been using this power. I had gotten tired, and come to see myself as an archival item more than an archivist: weak, crumbling, and in need of a very specific environment to survive. My pencil and my teeth and my sense of smell felt sharpened now, by loss and adversity and love. I moved confidently through the work.

And it was working. The first night nothing changed; we mopped the floor, we wrote by the light of our phones, we endured the harsh air, full of the hot ragged edges of dying papers. But by the end of the second night, the air was lighter, and a breeze seemed to sweep the stacks. We both noticed it, felt it, and Florence sat back and cracked her wrist and said, "I think you're right."

"Well, there are more things in heaven and earth."

"Do you think she knows we're here?"

"I have no idea," I said. "But while I believe at this point that some kind of life-matter goes on after we're dead, I have to be honest: I don't think a personality or a consciousness can. That just seems too nuts. And Elsie has told me Tracy wouldn't hurt anyone—she was sort of a blank of a person, and compulsive about sex and romance in ways that sound exhausting, but she wasn't someone who'd want to damage people's things and scare them."

"People are worse than they look, though," said Florence. "So much worse. Most of us have all sorts of things we're capable of—that we'd just never tell anyone."

"If we're really capable of them, I think we would tell someone. By our words or our actions. If a thought stays a thought, it's just a thought."

"Most of *my* thoughts don't stay thoughts."

"You may be unusual in that. I personally have all kinds of awful thoughts that I don't do anything about, and never will. They don't mean I'm secretly malevolent or evil. They're just ordinary shitty thoughts, intrusive ones, that everybody has."

"Then maybe what persists after we die is whatever's in

our intrusive thoughts," said Florence. "Because I think that steady crackle of evil is the very heart of what we are as a species, and if we think the surface of us is anything other than a thin membrane keeping us from exploding at people, we're wrong."

"It might be," I said. "Monsters from the id."

"Exactly."

"It's in *Forbidden Planet*."

"It's also a totally accurate description of the id."

"I think I'm done for the night," I said, and pushed myself up from the table.

"Sol," said Florence, looking ahead of her at an invisible point on the wall, "the weird thing is, I think this woman and I were a lot alike."

"Maybe you were," I said. I didn't sit, didn't leave, just stood at the edge of the table with my chair pushed out.

"She was a lot," said Florence uncertainly. "And . . . I know I can be a lot too. It comes from having been made to be little, for so many years. I was married to Jack, and—you know, I was a children's librarian. Me."

"All that 'a lot' has to go somewhere."

"But you get that sort of cockiness when you don't really like yourself. People follow you because you seem confident, but you're not confident, not really."

"No."

"But we were also really different," Florence went on, and sighed. "I think she wanted to be a guy. Don't you?"

"There's wanting to be a guy," I said. "And there's not wanting to be a woman. And there's actually feeling yourself to be a guy, or someone who's not a woman. They're all really different, and complicated. Especially when you feel yourself to be a guy, but don't want to be one. Or when you feel yourself to be one, but you don't know it, and you don't even know why you always feel like you're pretending."

"Which one were you?"

"I was the last one. Of course."

"I can't even imagine what it's like," she said. "I used to want so much not to be a woman. But I can't imagine not being one."

"I know," I said, and knew I sounded testy. "There are so many directions you can take that desire. I think—I can't know—that Tracy chose none of them, and that's why she was unhappy."

"That's glib."

"Maybe it is. Like I said, you can't know."

"I think it abdicates an important responsibility—as an archivist—to say you can't know."

"I think it's our most *important* responsibility. And, Florence, I really do have to go. The sun's up soon. But I have to say, as archivists, we let people down when we pretend to be objective. We help them when we admit what we don't know. And those can look like the same thing, but they're opposite things."

"The sun," she said, and looked up at me with a flash of anger, "sure helps you to get the last word, doesn't it? It must be nice to have the odds stacked so that you can say, *If I don't get the last word here, I'll literally die.*"

"Not really," I said, gathering my things. "It sucks, actually."

"Is that a pun?"

"Nope."

The third night we started early, right at sunset on Sunday, because we still had twenty boxes to go, even with strictly minimal processing. Florence zipped through labeling folders while I put them in order; then we switched; then I started writing the finding aid. By then it was past three, and I was not surprised when Florence stopped by my desk, partway through returning the boxes to the shelves, and said she was going home.

"Thank you," I said. "You've done phenomenally."

"It's just that I'm exhausted. You don't need sleep like I do."

"That's true." I stumbled up from my chair—I hadn't been able to rest in the storage unit, with its fragile eyelid of metal between me and the partially sunlit hallway. I held out my hand. "Still—thank you very much."

She didn't shake it, but stood there twisting her own hands in each other. Her face in the fluorescent light was pale and soft, with a sweaty, pearly sheen. I dropped my hand and she gave a little cry, and said, "I'm sorry."

"For what?"

"I can't do it. You disgust me."

"Well, why in God's name do I disgust you," I said, and involuntarily I glanced at the clock: only a few hours left, and most of the writing was still undone.

"I don't trust you with this argument. You won't listen, you won't understand, and you won't agree. All that's going to happen is that I'll get upset, and you won't—"

"You just won't see how I'm upset," I said. "But this is pointless. I'm sorry I forced the issue."

"That's what it is, though," she said. "Sol, you always force the issue. I can't put it any better than that. You were right about the—ghost, or whatever this is, the life that's left behind. All of it. Figuring it out was probably easier for you than it would have been for anyone else. And that's all I have to say or will ever have to say. Did you take everything out of your office?"

"I did."

"You'd better double-check. And Marcelle will be back soon—she'll call you about any handoff stuff that happens." She was speaking rapidly now, her face seeming to clear, to coalesce. "I'm going to call in sick tomorrow. And I'll finish moving these boxes, but I'm just going to leave at that point. I don't want to talk to you ever again."

"That will do," I said. "Thank you again for your help."

I sat writing the finding aid until about an hour before dawn. A finding aid—if you've never read one, you should. They're count-up poetry, a kind of formal sonnet of information. Creator. Copyright holder. Language of materials. Extent. Scope and contents.

And the biographical/historical note, five hundred or a

thousand words summing up the collection's subject. If it's a person, you shouldn't try to capture the pith here. You shouldn't flash your psychological insight, like a diamond ring worn with the stone turned to the palm. You are a functionary, writing a report.

But you are allowed to explain why the collection is interesting. This is the solo of archiving. It is the Linus spotlight. I wrote:

Tracy Britton was an American television writer and producer, best known for the series Feet of Clay *(1994–1998). Britton was born in Los Angeles, the child of the screenwriter couple Michael and Damia Britton. Educated at the University of Southern California, Britton first rose to prominence as a writer of several episodes of* Star Trek: The Next Generation *and* Star Trek: Voyager. *As a result of connections made during the production of* Star Trek—*a success, despite Britton's presence as a gender-nonconforming, lesbian-identified writer in largely white, straight, and male writers' rooms—Britton was given carte blanche to write and produce* Feet of Clay, *an experimental science fiction series taking place aboard a space station threatened by aliens called the miha, and notable for its focus on the crew's psychological lives.*

Many viewers have interpreted Britton's work as LGBTQ-coded, especially the relationships between characters in Feet of Clay, *two of whom were played by gay or lesbian actors. The queer content of the show was largely subtextual, similar to queer coding on contemporaneous series such as* Xena: Warrior Princess; *fans did not know that the actors were queer, or that Britton was. In many cases they were under the impression that Britton—whose work was credited to the nickname "Trace"—was a cisgender man. Despite this, the series is important in the history of science fiction for its portrayal of queer identity.*

After the end of Feet of Clay, *Britton went on to write episodes of* Star Trek: Enterprise, Andromeda, *and* Battlestar Galactica, *but never worked in a managerial position in television again, as* Feet of Clay *was considered a financial and artistic disappointment. Britton also wrote several complete and fragmentary novels, including one based in the* Feet of Clay *universe and concluding its story. These materials were never published, but drafts are included in this collection. Britton died in 2018 at the age of fifty-eight.*

I checked my phone, almost ready to upload the finding aid and leave for the night. There was an email from Elsie.

Dearest chuck, are you ready for me to applaud the deed yet?? I am missing you, and your gentle touch. I'm going to be released from the hospital tonight, but won't be able to drive home, and they have asked for me to be released c/o a friend or family who can see me safely home and make sure I'm cared for. Will you be c/o friend or family? Are you done with the archives for now? I love you. My house doesn't have a basement, but there is a windowless storage room which we can make safe for you tonight. After that, we will see what you want to do. I'm sure it's better than living in your storage unit. Please come see me, in any case, and we can talk & fuck. I miss you more than I've ever missed someone I've only just met.

Yours (really),

Else (they/them)

Before I left the archives, I made a hasty change to the finding aid and uploaded it to the Online Archive of California:

Donation Information: Donated in 2018 by Else Maine.

It was time to go; I zipped up my bag and put it over my shoulder. No time for a sentimental last glance, but you don't need a last glance when you've memorized every inch of a space the way I had, every dust ball, every box that doesn't quite fit on the shelves, every slick untrodden spot in the corner of the bathroom floor, where the mop goes but no feet do. I could recreate the Historical Society of Northern California archives from memory if I had to, but only the outsides of them, as hollow as a blown-out egg. The boxes, but not what's inside. A husk or a shell of the place I loved most.

"I'm sorry I didn't listen more," I said aloud, and I left.

It was a five-minute walk to my storage unit and twenty minutes to first light. I stopped at a Peet's, perfumed with acrid coffee, and bought my last latte of the day, the first latte of everyone else's, and I thought of how that word *else* would now never mean what it used to mean.

And I thought again of the way they'd looked on our first date, and of something I'd said in college, before I'd known anything about myself: "I don't have a thing for women in corsets—I have a thing for women who *own* corsets." Else isn't a woman, but they're enough like those women to raise a velvet frisson on the backs of my knuckles, which have all grown out into hair but are still more Velcro than velvet.

I love that kind of person. It's their combination of anxiety with unselfconsciousness, a hunger for a beauty that's sincere, that's unmediated, or rather that's so mediated—all sugar and spice and MSG—that the taste for it can only be unironic. That's why I was afraid of this kind of person too: the fear of real emotion, and the recognition that my own commitments are different, fainter, with shallower roots.

I drank half of my cloying drink—syrup and clover—on the way into the storage unit. I rang down the door with ten minutes to go until first light. I lay down on the blanket on the floor and went to sleep, and I wondered if the steady light and the draining of smell in the archives had meant that Tracy was satisfied, or if it was possible for Tracy to be.

CHAPTER 25

The Spirits Did It
All in One Night

How are you, my friend?

This is Alice again.

i'm good

alice, we processed the collection from my partner's ex this weekend

it was huge

Really! How huge?

106 linear feet

And the spirits did it all in one night!

sick, right?

i mean, very good!

I know slang, Sol!

I work at a college!

(/live/am—I exist at a college)

but what i was going to tell you is that i think it healed the eidolism

i think eidolism can be healed by effective processing and cataloging

"finishes the business"

shows care

calms emotions

i've been talking about it extensively with a colleague

all the signs have reversed themselves

Are you KIDDING?????

no

i have a better sense of humor than that

I'm not saying you're wrong, but I cared very much for my archives, and eidolism still destroyed them.

I processed all day and all night. I was a processing monster. It didn't save them.

i know you did, and do, and were

but i bet you still never got through backlog

LOL, no.

You're telling me some collections are more haunted than others.

i am telling you that!

in my case, it was very obvious, because things accelerated when this collection came, and because i was around 24/7

but i also think I must have a good instinct for this

something about me just knew where to aim

An archivist stands and falls on their instincts, yes.

shame

anxiety

injustice

unfinished business

you wouldn't believe the shit that i saw

mold

sap

the tv shorted out

I need to think about this.

Believe it or not, it never occurred to me that eidolism could have a cause outside of me and my body.

I didn't know about it until it was too late, because I didn't use Facebook—I guess they also had a listserv before that, but I never paid attention even to the listservs I was on.

Are you able to come here?

I can't even imagine what the logistics would be!

But think about it.

I would love your help.

Also we could write a paper!!

i'll think about it!

phone is dying

but let me get back to you

When the phone shut down, I played my keyboard through headphones, by touch, until the batteries ran out. Then I played it silently and tried to hear the music in my head, but I kept losing my spot in the dark—finding myself in sideways pianos, dream-pianos, where the black keys are in the wrong places and nothing makes any noise. By six o'clock I was starting to hallucinate fine beveled lines like toothpicks in the air. Just because I can't look at the sun doesn't mean that I'm any better at handling complete darkness. My head ached, and I unrolled the door of the storage unit aware that I was covered in my strange oleaginous sweat.

Outside in the cool December air, underdressed in a black tank top and with my keyboard and a bag under my arms, I felt a little better. I was halfway to Saint Francis before I remembered that I was due for a blood transfusion tonight, and wouldn't be able to get one in Marin if I stayed for a while, so I turned back and laid the keyboard awkwardly up against the wall of the clinic. The chairs were empty tonight. Ari was on duty, and he came out of his little office pulling at his beard, which he'd bleached blond along with his hair. It was dry and foamy now.

"Eighth night," he said. "Came to light the candles with me?"

I'd forgotten even what time of year it was. Only after he went back to the office and brandished the menorah at me, with its eight candles like sword points, did I remember. Tenderly I leaned down in front of it while he held the shammes steady, both of us singing the same blessing to different tunes. Then he hooked me up and sat in the recliner next to me as my phone charged.

"How're you doing, pal?" he asked comfortably.

"I'm good," I said. "I got fired."

"You hated your job, if I recall."

"I loved my job, but I hated the people there. Some deserved it, some didn't. But I don't anymore. It's like a—a pressure that got released, and now I don't hate anybody anymore."

"If you hate the people, you hate the job."

"I loved the dead ones," I said. "We had more in common, anyway."

"I definitely work here because I like vampires better than people," said Ari. "I mean better than living people, sorry."

"I know what you mean. I'm not really people."

"You absolutely are. You're a real fuckin' person, man. I shouldn't have said that. So where to now?"

"I don't know," I said. "I had a responsible job. It's a competitive field. It's also a tiny one, where rumors travel fast, so I don't really know if I'll work in it again. I don't know if it's right for me to. But it's hard to imagine living without it."

"Living? That's a strong word."

"I also know we just talked about this. But you can't imagine what a privilege it is to take care of ghosts. Even before I spent a lot of time thinking about dead people, and maybe people who are technically undead, I was well aware that it was my job to take care of ghosts. And that suited me fine. I always was sort of best with imaginary or fictitious people, Ari. I was a fanfic writer."

"Every trans man."

"I know. But I was also a musician. My job was always to sort of push ghosts out of the piano—to re-create voices that have gone silent. The piano is the most amazing device for bringing people back from the dead. People used it to transmit their voices down through history—piano and sheet music, that's all you need—long before there were ever recordings. It simulates a *whole* voice, a complete voice, a kind of voice that you can't sound out without getting several people together. And that voice can sing anything you can imagine. I've never been that good at talking to people, Ari, but I've always been real good at channeling."

"How the fuck is that true? You're obviously good at talking to people."

"I guess I mean—sure, I'm good with words. But I never learned to *work* with people outside of my mind, and yet I'm still around. I mean, I'm dead, but not because of that. I think I'm okay with the way that I am. I just need to figure out a way to fit it into the world a little better."

"I've never heard you say you're dead before."

"We just met. But it's true that I don't say it that often. Maybe I should. Do the vampires you work with say it? And why do you like vampires better than people?"

"The older ones say it more, for some reason," said Ari, stroking a key on the computer that showed my pulse and blood pressure readouts to keep it from falling asleep. "'Since I died.' I mean, not the people who'd been vampires longer—the ones who had lived longer when they started."

"Makes sense."

"I suppose it must. And as to why—" He closed his eyes, let his face slacken. The flickering from the menorah was loud and orange in the hall, looking like a projection onto the stage at a play. "A non-asshole way to put it? Not 'your problems are realer,' or something. No, it's just that as a nurse—"

"Very transmasculine occupation."

"Terribly. We learned to care for people because it stopped us from looking at ourselves, and because it felt like we were womaning right, isn't that true? But as a nurse, I'd rather care for people who are in the most immediate kind of need. Same reason some people like to work in obstetrics. People come in, I heal them, they're better. They're in real danger before I do it, and less danger after. I don't like to hang out with people either. I don't like to perform. I don't like bedside manner. I like to light my candles and chat when I feel like it, like when I see another trans guy who seems to be having a bad day. I just like to heal and go. That feels honest and it feels frank. It's more dignified for my patients. I think that if you can just quietly help, you should."

"Yeah," I said, and put my hand on his arm for a moment.

I was more nervous about seeing Else than I thought I would be. I still felt that being with other mascs made me feel small, overmastered, feminine. That's not right or fair, I know it's even homophobic in me, but I can't help my instincts, or the dry-skin taste they leave on my tongue. And while playing at boys had been fun, having Else tell me to use this name felt like a step that wouldn't be taken back, and that I had to take seriously. I knew that knowing Else would always be fresh like that, that there would not come a time when we were domestic, when I knew them so well that I could fake and fumble my way through a day together.

They came out of the hospital door, and I leaned my keyboard against a pillar and bent up to give them a kiss. My hands cupping their smooth warm face were very aware of the heat—like warming at a fire, like protecting a candle.

"Else," I said, and it was easy. I didn't need the fear and I didn't need the reassurance, the talk of domesticity, that had felt so important a minute ago.

"Is it stupid?"

"Not at all. It's extra," I said, savoring the word.

"I liked my name," they said. "I like that 'Else' says the quiet part of it loud. Is that what being extra means?"

"I think it's supposed to be an insult, but I never heard a queer person say it that way." I took their hand. "Let's go."

CHAPTER 26

A Totally Serious Person

The gray light from streetlamps whipped through the car. We were over the bridge now and in San Rafael, very close to home. I dozed on and off, the car passing through thin and thick layers of sleep, and when we got to the house Else practically had to carry me in. They opened the door and sighed into the dusty foyer.

"I feel like I've been away for months."

"You love this house, huh?"

"Would never leave it. Let's make up your room before we do anything else. I want you to be warm and comfortable."

The storage room was irregularly shaped, up a small and nonsensical flight of stairs, with three different heights to the ceiling. One alcove held an ancient fax machine, another an ancient printer. Else said, "This was Tracy's command center, when she was still writing for TV sometimes. Not her office, but where all the machines lived. There used to be racks of old *Feet* tie-in novels in here that never sold. I donated most of them a while back."

"Did you read her whole *Feet* book?"

"Yeah, did you?"

"Bits of it. While I was processing. It was—so bad."

"I know."

"Not even interestingly bad. I thought, oh my God, holy grail. But I was wrong."

"The holy grail. And Tracy was the Fisher King," said Else, disappearing down the stairs; I heard the rustling of sheets in the linen closet. "Wounded in the groin, can't get out of the boat, waiting for the healing words."

"You give her too much dignity."

"No, she really was just like that. A totally serious person. Will you pull this cot up for me? I'm not supposed to exert myself."

I brought the cot up into the room and unfolded it, and we made the bed together. The door of the room was thick and substantial, with rubber underneath. I said, "With electrician's tape, I think I could make that thing safe easy."

"And I'll spend the day with you in here."

"You'll need to eat."

"I'll bring peanut butter and bread and honey and water. I don't want to spend the day alone. I can get some writing done."

"Are you writing?"

"Yeah."

"Tell me it's slash."

"It's a memoir. God help me." They gave me a beady, careful glance. "It's slash, too. It'll be a strange book. But it's about time that I wrote my side of things."

That night we made a bonfire in the yard and burned a lot of Tracy's clothes. They were the kinds of clothes that burn, rather than the kinds of clothes that melt; flannels that went up in businesslike fashion, crisp and dry, and some unfashionable jeans. The clothes were bigger than I expected, and I realized that my image of Tracy was only current up to 1994, when she'd been a coat-racky dyke with softball arms. Else showed me a photo, and I took it in my bare hand, feeling its slight greasiness. Else, seated, in a white armchair, in a white lace dress with a keyhole neckline; Tracy standing, in a cheaply made custom tuxedo with pants cut straight, so that to contain a woman's hips they needed to be much too wide at the ankle. Tracy late in life was solid and bearish, grizzled even, looking in the bloom of health, like a lumberjack. Glamorous in a totally different way from the softball butch, a dyke who owned binoculars and a loupe for fine soldering work, who could fix the proverbial car. Else took the photo back with a faint reflected gleam from the fire in their eye, and I said, actually alarmed, "Don't throw that in!"

"Oh, dear God, no. This was our vow renewal. Did I look like—"

"You absolutely did."

They tucked the photo into their bathrobe pocket. By now they were wearing a heavy wool men's robe, also ex-Tracy's from the look of it, the kind they used to make in the fifties and sixties, that's practically a coat. I put my arm up around their shoulders, and kissed their warm lips in the cold.

Else went to bed at midnight, in the taped-shut storage room with me, so that they could sleep in without sleeping too late to spend the day together. I played piano through the headphones for a long time, with my legs stretched out before me and my back very straight against the wall. It felt so good to play again—to stretch the joints of my knuckles, and to once more be aware of all the different ways my fingers could bend. My hands had grown a little in the past few years, on testosterone, and I found their span was a little longer and that I could play with more force.

When I finally looked up from the keyboard, it was toward three. I watched Else sleep for a moment in the weak light from my tablet, and then I got up and stole over to look at them. They had thrown the covers off and lay with their strong, hairy arm across their stomach. The hairs were long and dark, with pointed tips, and they lay straight like lines of ink. The breasts just killed me to see, clearly outlined against their V-neck T-shirt, nipples puckered and dark, and I knew that around each of the nipples was a swirl of longer and more bladelike hairs. I knew I couldn't see them forever, that Else had probably opened a Pandora's box now whose howling contents couldn't be ignored until their chest was flat. Else would look good that way too, the smooth aerodynamic chest coasting down, a chest like mine, with the same scarring as the marks left by corduroy. I would miss the old body, I knew, would have to find other things to stir up my desire like the foam on a wave, to boil me up inside. Would have to look harder, deeper. But nothing in life is permanent, you know, and nothing in love either. We love a body slipping through time, and we cherish it as time strips parts of it away, and we feel good until it slips away from us entirely. You can give up some things that give you pleasure, if it means the ones you love can have joy.

The house felt quiet, I realized. It felt as quiet and clean as a tree just felled. It felt empty of ghosts. I knelt by the bed and pressed my forehead to the edge of the mattress, and just as Else's waking hand caressed my shorn hair, the light on my tablet went out.

CHAPTER 27

Solus Rex

Florence emailed at midday:

Dear Sol,

After this, I won't talk to you again, but I wanted to let you know that your plan worked. The decay in the archives has stopped. The smell is better, and I've even noticed that there are little positive changes, too. I went to pull out a rusty staple in the Stephens papers earlier today, and the moment I put the remover under, all the rust flaked away and underneath was a clean staple. This happened several times, until I started just sort of tapping the sheaves of papers until the rust came out. I've never seen materials act like this. And the air seems colder, fresher, and purer, like there's a fan running in the window on a spring night. There just seems to be less pressure in the air, now that you're gone.

I will be blocking your email. Goodbye.

- - - - - - - - - - - - - - - - -
Florence Makowski
Assistant Archivist
Historical Society of Northern California
Pronouns: she/her/hers

When Else was better, we went into San Rafael together and bought a delivery van, hard-sided and windowless, with a wall between the seats and the back. Inside, we set up a lightproof grow tent meant for marijuana farmers. From the house, we hauled out pillows, blankets, books, a big flashlight, and the keyboard on its batteries, and when we were done, the reflective silver interior had become a sort of disco nest.

"Don't think it'll be too hot?"

"On the hottest days, maybe." I contemplated the quilted walls. "But it's winter now, and I'm just going to worry about one thing at a time."

"Keeping your goals simple is important," said Else. "But it's still ten hours to City of Industry."

"It's one mile at a time," I said. "And if I'm conservative about when I park and rest, it's not any different from driving to Marin."

"I guess not."

"The thing is," I said, "I got to a place where I was living in the basement at NorCal Historic by not taking any risks, and I got to be with you by taking them, so I'm going to keep taking them. This isn't going to be risky, just long and boring. I'll split it up into three nights instead of two. I'll park at the Walmarts where the RVs go."

"Sol," said Else, "I just worry about you. I want you to be safe."

"I'll be safe. I'm still a person who *hates* to not be safe." I embraced them, and they pulled me close, tucked the top of my head under their chin like a violinist or a mother bird. I touched their jawline with my fingertips. "This is going to feel amazing if you try T."

"Does the stubble get caught in people's hair?"

"I wouldn't know," I said. "I still can't grow a beard for one shit."

"I think I'll always be femme," they said thoughtfully. I felt the sweet vibration of their voice moving through my skull. "That's the funny part. I mean, not in dresses."

"Maybe. You seem to like dresses."

"Ah, no, I've just always looked hot in them, and I really just like it when people think I'm hot." They withdrew from me and sat down inside the van's back door. Today they had on a neutral sort of outfit, a black sweatshirt and black shorts made of the same material, and thick-soled Doc Martens, real shit-kickers. No makeup, and so I could see the beautiful velvet-gray that lines their eye sockets when they're tired, that perfect line of delineation between the socket and the cheekbone. Getting older is the most goth thing of all. "I so appreciate that you don't think this is weird, Sol."

"What's weird?"

"Standing here in this little outfit and saying I'm curious to try testosterone, actually. And I'll probably get my nails done when I come out of the psychiatrist's appointment."

"It's not weird to make your body yours," I said. "It's not weird to want a custom body. There are cis guys who are femme, and nobody ever tells 'em to just transition and be women, if they're going to show that limp wrist."

"How do I know it's the *right* custom body?"

"You try some things, and if you don't like them, you stop."

"It's such a terrible world," they said, twisting around to put their feet up. "So terrible for so many people, but I don't know why that means I can't try to be the person I fantasized about being when I was twenty-two."

"You never told me enough about that."

"Someone glamorous," they said, and their face lit up, a matte and diffuse light. "Someone science-fictional. Someone with a gender so advanced that nobody had even heard of it before. I don't know how that turned into 'witchy high femme.' The law of entropy, probably."

"And loneliness and eagerness to be loved," I said. "I mean, I get it. We default to what people like. But, Else, you should leave 'witchy high femmes' to the witchy high femmes. You're a hunk of a different matter."

"Yeah? You can tell?"

"You should see your face," I said. "You should see yourself talking about this. Use a mirror. You're the one who still can."

"Come up here," said Else. "Come up and let me hold you, before you go."

I suppose I'm an exorcist now. It doesn't feel like that—it feels like I'm still an archivist—except I'm hardly making any money, just what other people slip me under the table. But it's not that I really need money for anything but gas and a few clothes. I'm a trans man; I only shop at Uniqlo anyway, where the sleeves don't go down to my fingertips.

It did work, what Alice and I did in City of Industry. And then other things worked: the thing I did in Stockton, and then the thing I did downtown at the MOMA. And from there, other things have continued to work. I can identify the problems in an archives—the collections that are still raw, still full of unrealized anger or lust or curiosity—from a visit, now, sometimes several visits, sometimes just the catalog. I seek out eidolism—the lights, the scents, the whole upside-down church-basement service, and also the sense of familiarity and safety that means I am unsafe and among strangers. When I arrive, these ghosts quicken. I felt them in a hospital archives that had a radium-water jar and a whole room devoted to children's teeth. I felt them in the basement of a film vault under Berkeley, where hundred-year-old silver nitrate film is stored at forty degrees Fahrenheit to keep it from exploding. I even felt them in the little comics museum on the waterfront, a soft neutral space with no dangerous edges and a Starbucks nearby, but which turned out to have a small archives in the basement with unprocessed papers by Percy Crosby, who spent the last sixteen years of his life in psychiatric wards. I processed Crosby's papers in a night. Artists leave easy archives: manuscripts, letters, drawings. They usually know what's worth keeping and what's not.

Occasionally, I break in. Sometimes the person who alerts

me is a researcher, and I don't have a contact at the archives, and I don't get a response to my email about eidolism. It's still a fringe belief, and the more people understand it, the more precarious vampires' jobs become. But most of the time, I'm invited in, especially as my sense of where the trouble is gets more acute and I get better at my work. I feel it the most behind my right eye. I've been to most archives in the Bay now, many in Southern California and in Nevada and Oregon, and I've even been up—with Else—to Alaska, but I have never been back to the Historical Society of Northern California.

I stay out for a few days at a time. It's stressful to be out in the van, even with the grow tent inside. I sleep badly, and the reflections in the walls give me both dysmorphia and dysphoria. So every third day or so I spend in Marin, at Else's house. I like to time it as tight as I can, because it feels better when I take all the risks that are possible to take—when I cram as much life as possible into the small container I have. I usually pull up to the door around an hour before first light. Over the soft gravel of the access road, the van makes a low blur of white noise, and in the absolute darkness broken only by the city's smear of light on the horizon, I can see the lights of Else's house burning as bright as the sun.

Acknowledgments

Thank you to Victoria Savanh, who edited the book with style, humor, and élan. Working with her is like fencing with an Olympian—the swish of the rapier, the total control, and the glee of watching her nail it again and again. You're not losing; you're learning.

I am very grateful to my agent, Kate McKean, for seizing the book from slush and thumping it with an open palm until editors were drawn by the sound. Kate always makes me feel emphatically welcome in publishing, and she should be celebrated with her own holiday.

Thanks to Austen Osworth for valuable early notes on the manuscript, and to Dave Cole for superb copyediting. Sabrina Bowers gave the book its note-perfect internal design. A very special thanks to Calvin Kasulke for his help at every phase of writing, including informing me that what I had with "vampire archivist" was not a joke, but a book.

I would like to thank Aaron Fellman, Sarah Guldenbrein, Danny Lavery, Julian Jarboe, Erin Cashier, Fait Poms, and Calvin again for their love and support. Each of you has taught me something vital.